The Best and Wisest Man:
Being A Reprint of the Reminiscences of
Mrs. Mary Watson, née Morstan

By Hamish Crawford

Dear Dean,

I thank you so much for supporting my book. It has been a pleasure from beginning to end working alongside you — and learning from you — on It's a Wonderful Life. From that nosy neighbour to Martini (to trying not to crack up at the bathroom scene) each of your characters has been so enjoyable to see. And you're a terrific guy off-stage as well! Thanks again, keep in touch, and I'll let you know about 'Jive Clviah': The Musical'!

Best Wishes,

(TORQUIL.FINLAY @GMAIL.COM

Paperback ISBN 978-1-78092-739-8
ePub ISBN 978-1-78092-740-4
PDF ISBN 978-1-78092-741-1

Published in the UK by MX Publishing
335 Princess Park Manor, Royal Drive,
London, N11 3GX

www.mxpublishing.co.uk
Cover design by www.staunch.com

Acknowledgements

I'm at a phase in my life when I seem to be surrounded by couples. In its own way, this made the writing of this book somewhat easier. So (deep breath...), Lena & Matt, Mike & Sarah, Rebekah & James, Tristan & Ty, Steve & Ally, Ashley & Chris, and Fergus & Mariana: at so many times you've been unfailingly helpful, offering me everything from advice and encouragement to a place to stay during the sprawling writing process. I must also mention the first couple I ever met, my wonderful parents. Thank you all for allowing me to be the weird Sherlock Holmes intruding on various points in your relationships.

A grab bag of others: John Wrightson and Jon Graham supplied cigars and sympathy when needed; Kirk Ramdath, the best Poet Laureate Calgary has (so far) never had; Joe Bor, Zac Brewer, Michelle Brooks, Caroline Cooke, Rob Greens, Kevin Krisa, Alanna Remington (who bought more copies of my last book than many family members managed), Todd Sullivan, and filmmaker extraordinaire Darius De Andrade. And a special mention to Dustin Nelson, whose reply when I told him I was writing an epistolary novel gave me many laughs (and I couldn't repeat here).

Massive and specific thanks to Kenna Kelly-Turner, for reading over my work and offering invaluable comments.

The fact that I am not a demure Victorian 'New Woman' did not escape me in the writing process, making her perspective and formidable intelligence doubly appreciated (and those who know her know I'd have had to say that even if she didn't like it, so the fact that she did makes it easier). No doubt I've still snuck mistakes into the final version—call it a gift. Similarly, Steve Emecz has been unfailingly positive and supportive.

Most of this narrative was compiled with the aid of Leslie Klinger's *Annotated Sherlock Holmes*. If you only buy one book this year and you haven't stolen this one, I recommend you get it. Klinger's insights into the world of the Great Detective, and his enthusiastic entry into the spirit of its factual basis, were invaluable in the mishmash of Victorian fact and fiction that I've tried to create here. To all those scholars who have contributed to the many and varied writings of and about Sherlock Holmes—from Jay Finlay Christ to T.S. Blakeney—I owe a great debt and am privileged to be in your company. And to those who have recently regenerated the Holmes name—Steven Moffat and Mark Gatiss, sure, but also Guy Ritchie and Robert Doherty—thank you for reminding a wider audience just how enduringly brilliant Sir Arthur Conan Doyle's idea was. It's bracing to think that Cumberbatch and Miller— and yes, purists, even RDJ—have added shadings just as fascinating as Basil Rathbone and Jeremy Brett.

Finally, and perhaps most importantly for this particular book, I must thank Nicole Armstrong, who bought me a beautiful hardcover collection of all 60 Holmes stories for my birthday back in 1995.

Here's a relevant example of how fortunate I am in the friend tolerance department. You may recall in *Sherlock Holmes and the Voice of Terror* (1942), when Holmes (Basil Rathbone) reaches for his deerstalker, Watson (Nigel Bruce) remonstrates him and he dons a less conspicuous fedora instead. It may shock you, dear reader, to know that I own a few deerstalkers, and all the people I mentioned above have unfailingly allowed me to wear them in public. I'm always touched that they do.

Hamish Crawford

1926

"But is not all life pathetic and futile? Is not his story a microcosm of the whole? We reach. We grasp. And what is left in our hands? A shadow. Or worse than a shadow— misery."
— 'The Retired Colourman' (1926)

It was a dreary Sunday afternoon in November and Queen Anne Street was deserted. The engine of the green MG that pulled up outside the smart row of flats broke an otherwise eerie silence. The woman of thirty-five who stepped out of the car wore a dress of vivid yellow that contrasted sharply with the slate-tinted day. She set her eyes on the upstairs window of the office across the road, and saw a rustle of movement. She walked up to the black door, pressed the button a single time and was let inside by a sombrely attired secretary.

"You are expected, madam," he said blandly, not accepting the card she held out.

The rooms upstairs had clearly been unchanged since they were first occupied in 1902. Dustsheets covered most of the overstuffed furniture; another had only recently been removed from the heavy oak desk. The man who had been sitting behind it rose as she walked in, and slipped on a conservatively cut grey lounge jacket. He stood silently for just a second too long.

"Good afternoon, Father," the woman greeted him in as bland a voice as she could manage. She noticed his

1

face minutely crease at her lack of emotion, and he diffidently accepted her hand and shook it.

"Mary my dear ... how long has it been?"

She did not answer.

He resumed his seat, and she sat opposite him. He ordered his secretary to prepare some tea, and Mary leaned back and contemplated how little time had changed her father, Dr. John H. Watson.

Mary dutifully asked how his family was. She did hope Watson's current wife and two children were looked after, appreciated. She tried not to be bitter as she compared the circumstances to her own upbringing. However, the sedentary and sedate family man sitting across from her was clearly a more attentive parent, a better parent, than the restless adventurer she knew as a child. As they spoke, and drank Simmons's too-strong tea, the charm and warmth Mary remembered in him resurfaced. She considered why she had come here, and for that reason was glad he had warmed up so.

"What brings you to London, Father? You're not seeing patients, are you?"

With some enthusiasm Watson gestured to a pile of papers on the desk. "No, no. I've persuaded Arthur to go ahead with these—one last set of cases to be published. I am so glad he agreed, there are many fascinating cases in here. 'The Illustrious Client', 'The Problem of Thor Bridge' ... the *Strand* really want me to publish 'The Giant Rat of Sumatra' at last, but the world still isn't ready. Still, if I don't, I may have to run with that appalling Mazarin Stone.

Some cases can turn out decidedly inferior on the page, I've found." He paused, and shrugged in apology. "My dear, forgive me. I know these stories cannot be of much interest to a young person like you."

"On the contrary, I've always loved reading them."

"Yes, so many people do. I can't quite fathom how they continue to hold such a grip ... the world has changed so very much, and sometimes I wonder if they seem irrelevant."

"Of course not. I imagine people will keep reading them ... forever, probably."

"Now you're starting to sound like your mother." The crack in his voice told Mary everything she needed to know. Embarrassed, Watson cleared his throat and shrugged. Mary knew that the matter would be harder to discuss than she predicted.

"So this ... casebook of Sherlock Holmes will still have 'By Arthur Conan Doyle' written underneath it?" she continued. "It doesn't seem very fair to you."

"I *lived* these cases, Mary. That is all the credit I need." Mary shivered as he added, "My dear Mary ... that is, your mother ... always preferred my name left out anyway. You remember, she was always concerned with my reputation."

Mary tensed. This was the right time to mention it, to come to the point. But despite herself, she enjoyed seeing her father and did not know how he would react to the real purpose of her visit.

"I'm glad you've occupied him—Arthur Conan Doyle, that is—on something more worthwhile than fairies and spirits."

Watson tutted. "Spiritualism was always Arthur's pet subject. I remember when he first got interested in the subject—'psychic studies', he called them, as though that made them any more respectable. That was back in '86."

"Someone with his reputation carrying on like a crank, though."

"Now, Mary. I know he looks foolish. It's not the beliefs themselves—well, not entirely. I think it's the tenacity with which he preaches about them ... I can't begrudge my friend that though. After losing his son in the War ... I can well imagine what that does to someone."

He turned away from Mary for a moment, and she could see his features were clouded with emotion. How often, she wondered, did he think about her death? Was he thinking of it now?

Before she got to business, she had to add something. "Well, I do know that there can't be a person in the world who isn't thrilled at the prospect of more Sherlock Holmes stories. The last thing I saw before I set sail for America five years ago was an Eille Norwood film of 'The Red-Headed League' in Leicester Square; and when I got off the *Queen Mary*, there was John Barrymore starring as Holmes in Radio City."

Watson chuckled. "And Gillette's still on the stage you know. He's as old as I am, and he runs about with pistol in hand and that ridiculous deerstalker on his head. Unbelievable."

"In America everyone's obsessed with *The Jazz Singer*. A talking picture, they call it. Imagine how successful Holmes will be if everyone could hear him saying ... 'Elementary, my dear Watson', for instance."

"Damn it all, Mary, Gillette wrote that line!" Watson's whitening moustache arched into a hearty chuckle when he realized Mary was teasing him. "Does seem to be a catchy, er, phrase, as it were. Maybe it will outlive anything I ever wrote."

"Sometimes, when I see all of that, he doesn't seem like a real person. I don't know how to describe it, but it's rather like knowing your father was best friends with ... I don't know, Tarzan."

They both laughed, and Watson added, "Sometimes he didn't seem like a real person when I was sitting across from him in Baker Street. When I think of how angry Holmes would get, he would accuse *me* of demeaning his profession. I really can't imagine how he responds to seeing himself turn into a cowboy."

"Well, they're just fun films, Father."

"I can't fault that. But you know, I did start my writing with the intent of seriously celebrating Holmes's talents and instructing the reader in the business of crime-solving. But on the screen, there's hardly any detection or his science of deduction, they're just adventure stories with all the stunts and fighting. I'd like to ask him ..." Watson broke off, gripped with an unexpected strain of emotion.

Mary knew why, and she knew better than to ask him if they had met recently. Holmes had only gotten odder and even less sociable since he retired, and she was only too aware how Watson's new family regarded him: an anomaly, a relic from his old life. She thought back to that time she tried to see him, suddenly knowing that he would not want the pity of his old friend's grown daughter.

Suddenly, it seemed it was time.

"Father, I must be honest with you. This wasn't purely a social call." She looked away before his frown distracted her, and pulled a crumbling notebook from her bag. The object lit his face in recognition, although it was still commingled with the frown.

"It can't be ..."

"It was in the care of Mrs. Forrester. Her nephew recently discovered it in an unopened box of her possessions and thought I would like to have it."

Watson stood up abruptly and paced towards the window. The limp, from that ancient war wound in Afghanistan, struck him with exaggerated stiffness as he turned from his daughter. "I am sure you would. Please, do not feel you need to share its contents with me, after so long they cannot be of much interest—"

His sudden distance angered Mary, and she rose from her seat. "Father, I *would* like to share them with you. I cannot believe that, even though you have remarried, the thoughts of your first wife—of my *mother*—would be of so little interest to you." She stood next to him; he was clearly uncomfortable at the closeness. "Have you ever read this?"

6

"No," he said softly, keeping his gaze fixed out the window.

1888

"Well, and there is an end to our little drama," I
remarked, after we had sat some time smoking in silence. *"I
fear that it may be the last investigation in which I shall
have the chance of studying your methods. Miss Morstan
has done me the honour to accept me as a husband in
prospective."*

He gave the most dismal groan.

"I feared as much," said he. *"I really cannot
congratulate you."*

I was a little hurt.

*"Have you any reason to be dissatisfied with my
choice?"* I asked.

*"Not at all. I think she is one of the most charming
young ladies I have ever met and might have been most
useful in such work as we have been doing. She had a
decided genius that way; witness the way in which she
preserved that Agra plan from all the other papers of her
father. But love is an emotional thing, and whatever
emotional is opposed to that true, cold reason which I place
above all things. I should never marry myself, lest I bias my
judgement."*

—*The Sign of Four (1890)*

15 July—What odd fancies grip a young lady about
to be married! I have never in my life desired to write down
my thoughts, and yet now I am so filled with happiness I
feel compelled to note my every whim. I am sure James—

always recording his observations and his clues, and the brilliant things Mr. Holmes says—would say his habits are growing on his fiancée. Perhaps they have!

It may also be a result of the general upheaval the narrative of my life has lately seen. The passage of a month has seemed to make my former status quo a different lifetime entirely. It had frequently been observed, both from my dear employer Mrs. Forrester, and my good friend Kate Whitney, that my life had been heavy with losses. There was my mother's death when I was a child, my father Captain Arthur Morstan's sad disappearance, and the fact that I had reached the age of twenty-and-six still a spinster. Yet it would be wrong to dwell on such sadness when I had a great deal to be thankful for as well. I derived considerable satisfaction from my work as a governess; and Mrs. Forrester was so gentle and considerate an employer, and so hospitable a host from the moment I first lodged with her. Since I had lived in London, I could say with absolute candour that I did not consider myself an orphan with her love in my life.

More prosaically, since 1882 I had received a large and majestic pearl every 4th of May from an anonymous benefactor.

I will not dwell too much upon these events, and the connection with my father that they held, as they have been written up by James in the hope that they may be published[1]. One such case was published last year in

---

[1] These were ultimately published as *The Sign of Four* in *Lippincott's Magazine*, February 1890, and collected in book form later that year.

Beeton's Christmas Annual under the title *A Study in Scarlet*. But I feel it will better organize my thoughts to give a very brief sketch of the chain of events from my own perspective. This chain began with an innocuous conversation about the pearls one afternoon. Mrs. Forrester often teased me about my concern over my annual gift.

"Think of the brooches you could make with them. Or even a necklace—although given their size, you would need a far plumper neck! They'd look well on my neck, I dare say!" I laughed weakly, and she gave me a push with her stout arm. "Mary my dear, you must cheer up! Think what a blessing such beautiful jewels are! Titled ladies would consider themselves lucky to have a bauble half the size of one. And here you have six."

"I suppose it must be my nature," I sighed. "I think only of the potential calamity behind any boon that comes my way. It is ungrateful of me to entertain such gloomy thoughts, but it seems my lot in life."

"I had no idea you considered yourself so ill-fortuned," she replied.

"I only meant in this instance. I would consider myself more fortunate if I had my position as governess, your company, and no pearls to disconcert me."

"Life is full of hardships, as my late husband used to say."

Though I knew Mrs. Forrester was being sardonic, I had to qualify my anxieties.

"Take my father's disappearance, the very day after coming to London from those God-forsaken Andaman

Islands. I sometimes think some curse from that savage land took him away."

Seeing my anguish at these thoughts, Mrs. Forrester became serious. "Do you think these pearls have anything to do with that?"

I chuckled at this suggestion. "Perhaps that is somewhat far-fetched."

A thought struck Mrs. Forrester. "You know, Mary, about a year before we met, there was a domestic problem in this house. It was a baffling and tragic affair for all of us. My husband stood accused of … of poisoning one of the servants."

"Oh, my dear Mrs. Forrester!" I was quite shocked. Mrs. Forrester seemed far too unassuming of nature to have something so sensational happen to her.

She was quite sanguine at this recollection. "It was quite possible, Cecil had quite a temper and indeed a motive. I was at my wit's end, so I decided to enlist the services of a consulting detective." She smiled, though her description of the detective grew less and less flattering. "He was a very strange individual, not a gentleman by any means. When I think of when I went to his shabby room in Montague Street … how upset I was by him! He did not rise to greet me, and when I told him these details his eyes drifted closed. How dare this man, I thought. I ceased talking, stood up, and announced that I had never been treated so insolently in my life and I would leave. He replied that it was he who should be offended, my problem bored him immensely and he only took on such cases as

11

mine to ease his financial burden." She then paused and added, "I think you should talk to him."

"I shall do no such thing." I was horrified by her suggestion, which seemed like another joke but a very cruel one given my fragile state of mind.

"Why not?"

"He sounds like a horrible man," I said simply.

"At first I thought he was the worst man I had ever met," she agreed, "but watching him divine the true nature of the death—it is unseemly, I know, to see artistry in the unravelling of a gruesome event, but when he was at work, I felt privileged to see something so artistic. It was akin to seeing a mathematician solve a complex quadratic equation, or hearing Pablo de Sarasate's virtuoso skills on the violin. It was all to do with the pipes in our house—which have since all been replaced, by the way. They had introduced lead into the drinking water—"

"Please Mrs. Forrester, enough of this morbidity!"

"All right, but I beg you to consider seeing him. I wouldn't be surprised if he could solve your father's disappearance as well."

"Now I know you can't be serious. Not even the police could solve that."

"He is no policeman, I can assure you."

Despite Mrs. Forrester's endorsement, I was adamant that I had no need of any consultation. Perhaps such a course might uncover something terrible that was best undisturbed. It is strange how one's perspective could so radically alter, for though the events that I learned had led to my situation were indeed terrible, I feel myself far the richer for now knowing them.

As sometimes happens, providence will unwillingly prod one into action. On the morning of July 7, I received a letter. This may not seem an odd occurrence, but as I had no family and a very small circle of friends, I did not receive much correspondence. I remember thinking and hoping it might finally contain the news of my father I longed to hear. Despite my fervent hopes, it was in my nature to predict that whatever news it bore would not be good.

Nothing about this trivial yet uncanny piece of paper set my mind at rest. It was contained in an envelope of high quality. The paper within was of the finest, most luxurious feeling as well. My heart was light, and so the contents of the letter were doubly shocking.

It read: "Be at the third pillar from the left outside the Lyceum Theatre tonight at seven o'clock. If you are distrustful bring two friends. You are a wronged woman and shall have justice. Do not bring police. If you do it will be in vain. Your unknown friend."

I grew truly faint at this. The sentiment was technically noble, but I found it unsettling. The assignation had a sinister air to it, as did the warning about bringing police. It sounded, in truth, like the kind of missive a kidnapper would send in a penny-dreadful yarn. Yet the writer seemed to extend the possibility of friendship by claiming I was a wronged woman. Even then, the phrase was troubling. In what sense did the writer consider me 'wronged'? Did it concern my father? Or had the pearls been given to me in error?

I read these few words over and over, maddening myself trying to extract some subtext from them, something that might explain everything. By the time I gave up, I felt even worse. The prospect of meeting this stranger alone, no matter how beneficent his motives, filled me with the greatest dread. His qualification—that I may bring two friends—offered me little help. Mrs. Forrester was at that time visiting her family, and my only other close friend, Kate Whitney, had been called away to the hospital only the night before, as her husband Isa had taken ill. I could not ask her to leave the poor man's bedside to resolve some personal mystery of mine, no matter how fearfully I regarded it.

As for the other few friends I had—well, it was such an impropriety! What could I tell them to expect? Worse than the inconvenience, I might even endanger them by soliciting their help. The prospect of an evening rendezvous in the London streets this year inevitably carried an air of the most depraved horror about it. For even though Jack the Ripper would have been far from his grisly trade at the Lyceum, it still seemed like he might be anywhere, hidden in the night shadows, opera cloak and top hat concealing ghastly instruments of death.

The alternative was really the only one I could contemplate, such was my desperate train of thought. I would simply have to pay Mrs. Forrester's consulting detective a visit. I gathered everything that might be termed 'evidence' in my case: the letter, the pearls, and the letters that accompanied those objects, in the event that there might be a connection.

Mrs. Forrester wrote me with enthusiasm when I asked for her advice, but her telegram carried an air of smug thrill. She was, though, truly concerned for me, and had taken the trouble to inquire about him before she departed.

Telegram from Mrs. Cecil Forrester to Miss Mary Morstan

DELIGHTED TO HEAR. DETECTIVE'S ADDRESS NOW 221B BAKER STREET. WASTE NO MORE TIME.

It was not a part of London I had occasion to visit very often, and it did not occasion as much fear on my part as the letter had elicited.

I just imagined Mrs. Forrester's assurances as I prepared for my visit.

"The man is a professional, after all, so what is the worst that could happen?" I would have asked her.

"Exactly my dear," Mrs. Forrester would have said. "You'll thank me, I promise you."

Perhaps Mrs. Forrester exaggerated, and he would be a charming and welcoming gentleman who would accompany me this evening and protect me from any dangers I may face.

Perhaps behind that odd name—Sherlock Holmes—stood a chivalrous and noble knight in shining armour.

From all this strange turmoil, I was positively gripped with nerves when I called on Sherlock Holmes that afternoon. I remember my feelings so vividly as I alighted from the carriage to that careworn front door at Baker Street, as I entered the disarrayed sitting room and heard a resonant, curiously un-accented voice announce: "Please enter, and sit here by the fire."

My first impression was of Mr. Holmes was his enormous rounded head, and the pair of intense eyes that burned in my direction. He wore a frayed mouse-coloured dressing gown, and his soft-collared shirt, with a bowtie tucked underneath it, had a similarly negligent, bohemian appearance. I suppose I was somewhat surprised by this casual attire and lack of formality, but I thought little about it, as I was preoccupied with his unblinking, unwavering gaze directly at me. I felt rather like an unsuspecting herbivore entering the lion's den.

Had Holmes alone been there I may very well have turned on my heel and run out the door. But fortunately I surveyed this inhospitable environment nervously and locked eyes upon its other occupant. And as you may expect, more importantly than any of these details, etched into my mind is my first sight of my dear fiancé, James—or as I then knew him, Dr. John Watson.

How did I initially regard him? As I indicated, I was at first so overwhelmed with Holmes's predatory gaze that this other gentleman's presence barely registered. It was that sideways glance I cast him—that seemed, on my recollection, to last both an instant and an eternity—that is my strongest memory of this day. In contrast to his colleague, he stood up as I entered, and when I turned to him, I saw that he was looking upon me in a far more welcoming fashion. He was far more respectably clad, in a tweed lounge suit, a stiff upright collar, and black necktie. It is somewhat silly to write down, but I remember feeling particularly reassured by his moustache—a full but unobtrusive growth that carried to me the very essence of probity in its bristles.

When I am nervous, I am given to talk excessively. Holmes and Watson had both introduced themselves, I had taken a seat in front of the fireplace, and silence fell over the room. Fixed with Holmes's glare, my mind went blank, so I rattled off with some panic Mrs. Forrester's recommendation.

"I believe I was of some slight service to her. The case, however, as I remember it, was a simple one."

His voice was flat and emotionless, as though he was reading an encyclopaedia entry. I was surprised that the work he had done—that she had considered so positively miraculous—could affect him so little.

"She did not think so," I replied. "But at least you cannot say the same of mine. I can hardly imagine anything more strange, more utterly inexplicable, than the situation in which I find myself."

This statement, which I said with sadness and gravity, triggered—how should I describe it?—a sentiment very like glee in Holmes. He leaned forward in his chair, rubbed his hands together, and his eyes seemed to light up with enthusiasm. It was clearly visible that he had to physically contain any further enthusiasm. He resumed his curt and professional tone as he said, "State your case."

Watson at this point rose from his seat. "You will, I am sure, excuse me," he said.

I was filled with panic at the thought. I was desperate that he not depart! So with as much composure as I could muster, I said to Holmes: "If your friend would be good enough to stop, he might be of inestimable service to me."

(James has since told me of the informal arrangement of his assistance to Holmes. He often feels, he says, as though he is a spare and unwelcome presence in the room during some of the interviews.)

Holmes's arbitrary manners cooled to contempt as I laid the facts of the case. As I described the disappearance of my father, he interrupted my tears to clarify a date. Mrs. Forrester had left me unprepared—he seemed even more inhuman than she described.

In contrast to Holmes, Watson retained a courteous and polite interest in me.

Finally, I produced the letter. By this point I was not quite sure whether Holmes would accompany me—and if he did, whether his company would be any help. Once he read the letter, he asked me, "What do you intend to do, Miss Morstan?"

"That is exactly what I want to ask you," I replied. I felt like adding in some anger that I was quite at the end of my tether from all this, so did not rightly know what I should do.

"Then we shall most certainly go," he declared emphatically. "You and I and—yes, why Dr. Watson is the very man. Your correspondent said two friends. He and I have worked together before."

This suddenly made me anticipate this more keenly.

I asked Holmes sheepishly, "But would he come?"

He stepped between us, and once again I gazed at his kind eyes and his reassuring moustache. "I should be proud and happy if I can be of any service."

It somehow seemed that, with this plan in place, the atmosphere lightened. Though I suspect now that it was mainly in anticipation of his upcoming work, Holmes became more agreeable—he even paid me a compliment. When I produced the letters that accompanied the pearls, so he could compare the handwriting, he said, "You are certainly a model client."

It made me smile like a proud student.

From this interview, I descended from my stable life embroidered with puzzling details, down the rabbit's hole into a world where those puzzles were all that a rational mind could hold onto amid encroaching chaos. By the end of that very night we met the deeply eccentric man who had sent me the pearls, met a butler with whom Mr. Holmes had boxed, and then seen a dead body in a locked room.

Mrs. Forrester had not exaggerated Holmes's miraculous abilities. At the appointed hour, we met at the Lyceum, and from there we were transported by carriage from the Lyceum Theatre to the residence of Mr. Thaddeus Sholto in South London, and thence to the Sholto family home, Pondicherry Lodge, in Norwood. Throughout the journey, Holmes would not be silent, cataloguing each road we took—in spite of the metropolis around us being entirely shrouded in night's cloak. It was an impressive display, but it struck me as somewhat ostentatious. As I knew neither gentleman well, I half-suspected Holmes was trying to impress me with this skill. Watson in contrast remained silent, and I began to wonder whether he was shy or rude.

If I had thought Holmes eccentric, upon our arrival in South London, I saw that he was positively mundane compared to Thaddeus Sholto. This man had surrounded his humdrum lodgings with Indian trappings—from every corner hung tapestries and paintings. Thaddeus was keen to show off his connoisseurship, which was rather dubious to say the least (hanging next to artwork by Salvator Rosa, and a fine Corot, was a considerably inferior Bouguereau—perhaps to be fair to him, Thaddeus was merely a man of eclectic tastes). Every other available alcove seemed to have an ornate Oriental vase or *hookah* ignobly stuffed inside.

A prematurely bald man (albeit with a strange fringe of bright red hair) of thirty, with irregular yellow teeth, Thaddeus extended the air of gilded decay to himself, clad as he was in a silk kaftan and jewelled slippers.

It may seem waspish to remember the man this way—and in truth, in the unfolding of these events, I came to understand him as an honourable man, if not to like him. My initial impression of him, I must say, significantly suffered from the manner in which he related the death of my poor father, Captain Arthur Morstan.

It transpired that on that fateful night, my father had journeyed to Pondicherry to speak with Thaddeus's father Major John Sholto. Their conversation was about the Agra treasure, a fortune that had built Major Sholto's vast estate, and which by rights he ought to have shared with my father and two others. Thaddeus further explained that it turned to an argument, which aggravated my father's weak heart. Thaddeus was only told of this altercation at the elder Sholto's deathbed, when he also declared to his son that it was his intention to do right by me and restore my rightful share of the treasure Captain Morstan deserved. The secrecy of the gift was necessary as Thaddeus's twin brother Bartholomew, disapproved of including me in this way.

James—forgive me, for consistency's sake I should refer to him as Dr. Watson when I write of this period before our marriage—has since told me that at this point I looked very faint. I remember that he saw my distress and hurriedly handed me a glass of water. As I drank the water,

I tried to avoid becoming overly consumed with emotion by concentrating my gaze on Holmes. He leaned back in his chair with his eyes half-shut. His face had a bland look of distraction, and at that moment the stimulation he was getting from every macabre detail Thaddeus happily furnished him seemed very unsavoury.

I thought the tale Thaddeus had told me was strange and horrifying enough. Not only had my father been dead these ten years—something I had come to know in my heart, if not acknowledge—his final act in life had been the fruitless resolution of such mercenary business. For the price it had cost him, I had dearly wished he could have forgotten the treasure, no matter what he was owed, and never thought again about Major Sholto, no matter how unjust he was. It was not the last time I was forced to re-examine my father's conduct and wonder exactly how noble his actions had been.

In fact though, this strange horror was a mere overture for the night. Once we had reached Pondicherry, by which time it was already well past eleven at night, I knew there could be no turning back. For here, Thaddeus's twin brother Bartholomew lay murdered. I never set eyes on the ghastly sight—both of my companions immediately protected me from it. It was at that moment that I knew my worries about my benefactor were undoubtedly correct.

That evening afforded me the opportunity to witness first hand the contrast between the methods of Holmes and Watson and the official police. While Holmes, Watson, and Thaddeus Sholto investigated the locked room at the attic of Pondicherry, I waited downstairs with the maids. It was some time later that the police arrived, led by an exceptionally pompous and thuggish officer, Inspector Athelney Jones. He introduced himself to us brusquely and did not even pause for a statement before ascending to the house's attic.

"You may wish to know, sir, that Mister Thaddeus Sholto had involved Mister Holmes and Doctor Watson through myself," I informed him.

"Holmes? *Sherlock* Holmes?" Jones inquired.

"Indeed."

"Oh dear. The theorist, back to haunt me." The inspector in plain clothes accompanying him raised a sympathetic eyebrow, which suggested to me that Holmes was well known by these officers as 'the theorist', and that this name was by no means complimentary. "And I might have guessed that he would be depraved enough to involve … *ladies* in his sordid criminal investigations."

"On the contrary," I declared. "It is I who have involved him."

At an even greater loss for words, Jones sighed again and excused himself from our company. I never spoke with him again, something I cannot say I regret, other than for some resentment that he deemed my part in the story so incidental as to not merit a proper interview.

Later, I heard some testy exchanges between him and Holmes. It was at this point, overhearing the detective's dry appraisals of his professional counterpart, that I became firmly convinced that I had made the right decision putting my case in the hands of this man, and the dear Dr. Watson.

The remainder of the 'Sign of Four' case saw Holmes and Dr. Watson uncover a betrayal and robbery related to a treasure recovered at the Agra Fort in India. It was a dark tale rooted in greed, whose putative antagonist, a crippled ex-convict named Jonathan Small, was in many ways a misunderstood and sympathetic figure, despite his unrepentant murderousness. But for pity's sake, the man endured the loss of his legs by crocodile, a wrongful imprisonment, and a passage of years and decades without something that was owed him. I was convinced that it was the compound of these dreadful calamities, not any inherent vice, that had driven him to the fanatical villain who cast his shadow over the Sholtos. In a perverse way I was even grateful to this man, for it was through Small's account that I came to more fully understand that this background of corruption had eventually claimed the life of my father. It was not the hands of a savage curse that reached across to sunny England, but a thirst for lucre that was unmistakably English.

Once the detectives caught up with him, Mr. Small was quick to observe that my father's conduct was honourable. I shall always preserve the noble memory I have of him, and it is entirely unfair of me to judge his conduct from such a distance, and so many years after the fact. Nevertheless, the way that he and his fellow officers seized treasure for themselves left me ill at ease. True, it was treasure that Small and three Sikhs had themselves claimed from an unsuspecting Raj. But throughout the affair, Small—in spite of his uncouth manner and criminal preoccupation—had demonstrated loyalty and fidelity to his confederates, whether black or white-skinned. By contrast, the English officers and gentlemen—Major Sholto chief among them—grasped at treasure as though it was their birthright, and betrayed the trust of someone who had expected better of them. My father was, I have come to feel sure, not guilty of anything of that magnitude, but once again I was moved to consider how naïve my impressions were of noble Englishmen bringing peace and security to benighted colonies.

Oh dear, I am becoming submerged in irrelevant ruminations. These are all thoughts that have grown in me since the conclusion of the case. Between our initial journey to meet the Sholtos and the account from Mr. Small that concluded this tale, I remained at home while Holmes and Dr. Watson went about their investigations. No doubt my sex by default precluded me from participating in the rigours of this adventure. I dare say even Holmes possessed enough sensitivity and proper gentlemanly conduct to deem matters of murder and boat-pursuit unsuitable for a lady to be involved in. However, in my marrow I was somewhat saddened to be left out of the men's work. As several days passed, I came to think that I would enjoy any excuse to spend more time with Dr. Watson.

I contented myself with my lessons, though the students had now conspired to add to my torpor with unruly behaviour. Seeing me gaze out the window wistfully instead of looking over one child's handwriting exercises, Mrs. Forrester guessed the cause of my distraction.

"It's Sherlock Holmes, isn't it? I knew you would find him fascinating, and he is an appropriate age for a lady like you as well."

"Mrs. Forrester!" I cried. "Surely you did not send me to this detective merely to … affiance me? And Mr. Holmes to boot!"

"Do you not find him an eligible bachelor?" she asked. "If anyone could melt his stoic exterior, I am sure it would be you, my dear."

I shook my head. "There must be a stronger word than 'stoic' for Mr. Holmes's exterior. I find him an interesting and stimulating mind, but certainly not a suitor. It is too late, anyway, for a woman of my age to think of marriage. I am perfectly happy without it."

"My dear Mary, methinks you doth protest too much."

It was a well-worn quotation, but I could not deny its truth. After some prodding, I finally admitted, "It was his friend Watson I thought of." As soon as I had said the words, I felt very foolish.

"Watson? Holmes worked on my case alone. Is this Watson a detective as well?"

"He is a doctor who assists Holmes. They are so unlike—he is quiet and observes everything. Whereas Holmes is always talking and demonstrating his brilliance, the doctor stands on the sidelines." Now I had started, I could not stop talking about Watson's admirable features. I must confess I even said, "He is far more handsome than Holmes as well. He has a very distinguished moustache."

Mrs. Forrester found this gossip grandiloquently amusing. "Had I only known a simple soup-strainer would melt your heart! Cecil's friends have all manner of vile handlebars."

"Oh, Mrs. Forrester, he is a truly special man. He is so polite and pleasant to me, such a decent and courteous gentleman ..." I could not continue, for I had blushed.

"Doesn't sound nearly as interesting as Holmes, I must say," Mrs. Forrester opined.

"Well then, you may marry Holmes," I concluded, and we both collapsed into laughter at the prospect.

Though they were few and far between, opportunities nevertheless arose to get to know dear Watson better. He relaxed considerably, and I inferred from his manner that he had been a long time out of the company of women.

For all I anticipated our time together and enjoyed his company when he came to me, every moment carried with it the tinge of sadness. At this stage, after all, he was primarily interested in the mystery. I was merely a paying client to him and his colleague. I worried that my possible interest might breach some professional code of ethics. Furthermore, perhaps he would regard my interest as a mere infatuation. I thought of Mrs. Forrester—as amusing as she was, there was something perhaps partly tragic about her interest in Holmes. Though she concealed it in badinage, there was clearly a longing that she felt since her husband Cecil's death. When I mentioned her name to Holmes when we first met, he betrayed only the briefest flicker of recognition. His passion was reserved for the specifics of her case. She was, to him, no more real or interesting than an encyclopaedia entry.

My second worry concerned the outcome of this investigation. I stood to gain a quarter-share of an incredible fortune, according to Thaddeus Sholto. From the beginning I knew Watson was a gentleman through and through—something I could not certainly say of Holmes. But his credentials were a source of sadness as well, as I knew he would never deviate from the peculiar code that governs such persons' actions. When I gained my wealth, such a man would immediately feel unable to continue making my acquaintance, as he would be unable to match my newfound wealth and style of life.

Oh, how long I pondered that! More than pondering, even; I agonized over its complications. I tried to think of a way around it, a way to tell this dear man that he need not feel bound by such abstract concerns. Once again, the petty business of money, which had claimed my father, was now to take another dear man away from me.

I confess, though, that contemplating such matters had left me particularly melancholy, when late one evening, the servant entered the drawing-room and told me, "There is a Doctor John Watson at the door, ma'am. He is accompanied by a policeman."

"Show him in."

The servant impudently arched an eyebrow in judgement. The hour was far too late to admit such a visitor, and it occurred to me that the fellow thought any man in the company of a police inspector must be on the wrong side of the law. I was happy to see Watson at any hour, even if he was thought to be a criminal.

As he entered, I took shelter in the corner of the drawing-room, in a convenient basket-chair. I had taken little care of my appearance, not anticipating gentleman callers, and so I dimmed all lights in the room save a shaded lamp next to the basket-chair, lest he see the melancholy etched into my face.

It caused me some amusement to see him appear before me. I could well imagine the poor servant's incredulity. Frankly, he looked an utter mess. His smart Chesterfield overcoat was flecked with daubs of oil and heavy patches of gunpowder, the sleeves were ripped, and the lapels were bent inwards. He carried with him a peculiar piscine smell, and the bowler hat he handed to the servant was punctured.

Seeing him standing there, nervousness re-entered my demeanour. I was suddenly struck by the realization that after my protracted longing that we might share some time alone together, this was the first time we had done so.

My worry at this caused me to become quite garrulous: "I heard a cab drive up. I thought Mrs. Forrester had come back early, but I never dreamed it might be you. What news have you brought me?"

In writing this conversation, I am aware now that I sounded positively cold with him. This was not in any way sincere, but was merely my way of defending myself against the inevitable heartbreak I seemed destined for.

"I have brought something better than news," he declared. "I have brought something which is worth all the news in the world. I have brought you a fortune."

He was full of good cheer, and for his sake I smiled and nodded indulgently. But as I looked down at that box, I could only see the object that would stand between this wonderful man and me.

"Is that the treasure then?" I asked coolly.

My bland response somewhat surprised him. "Yes, this is the great Agra treasure," he grandly confirmed. "Half of it is yours and half is Thaddeus Sholto's." After this, he launched into somewhat pedantic detail about the great benefit it would bring to me. I could not listen, though, because the prospect of such a life ahead of me seemed so dreary.

So, when Watson had finished speaking, I shook my head at his childlike enthusiasm and tried to respond without betraying my feelings. "If I have it, I owe it to you."

Watson looked away from me, and his bluster continued. "No, no, not to me, but to my friend Sherlock Holmes. With all the will in the world, I could never have followed up a clue which has taxed even his analytical genius. As it was, we very nearly lost it at the last moment."

Consumed with grief over our imminent farewell, I contained myself and showed no emotion when he outlined the various avenues of his investigation. All of it—the clever dog Toby following a scent, only to be distracted by the smell of creosote, Holmes uncovering the path of the boat *Aurora*, his disguise as an aged maritime man, even a chase down the Thames with ample pistol fire exchanged—passed me in growing disinterest. I cringe now as I think of poor James—poor Watson, rather—squirming in discomfort, thinking my disinterest was with him. That he could think I viewed this conversation a dull prelude to recovering my birthright! No sentiment could have been farther from the truth.

I was brought resoundingly back to the conversation, though, when he casually added, "The poison dart came within an inch of us."

"Did you say a *poison* dart?"

"Oh yes," he said airily. "Wielded by Tonga, the Andaman Islander who assisted Small."

His mention of a near-death experience—and the way he casually said it, giving it no more thought than the stripes painted to disguise the *Aurora*—made me feel very faint. He dashed to my side with a glass of water, and I attempted to shrug it off. "Forgive me, Miss Morstan, I sometimes get carried away with these gloomy details."

"Details? More than a detail, I think. To think that you could have been killed!"

"But I was not," he replied, "So I do not think of it."

I must admit that this statement struck me as rather foolish. Now that we have told each other so much about ourselves, and I came to know exactly how many times he had faced death, that I understood how essential this *laissez-faire* outlook was.

At the time though, he returned to talk of the treasure. I grew downright irritated with him when he said, "I got leave to bring it with me, thinking that it would interest you to be the first to see it."

Only for his sake did I muster some interest and reply, "It would be of the greatest interest to me." I knew well from my students that such superlative statements tend to sound sarcastic when said in this way, and Watson's raised eyebrow told me he was very confused by my reactions. Admittedly, I was somewhat interested in the elaborate Indian carvings on the box ("Benares metal-work," Watson explained). As the key had been thrown into the Thames during their pursuit, Watson then needed to force the box open with a nearby poker.

My heart was in my hands as the box snapped open. It was completely empty! Its weight was entirely due to that iron casing, which was an inch thick. We stood in silence, looking down at it. I could not think of anything to say—after all the trouble he and Holmes had taken to retrieve this, I imagined Watson would feel that he had failed. I thought he would be very bitter indeed—that his days of work had borne no fruit, and that he had nearly been killed over an empty box!

"The treasure is lost," I stated. It instantly seemed fatuous, but I could think of no other comment to make.

I looked across, and saw a curious transformation. Watson's earlier animation dropped away, and he became for a second quite still. Then he stepped back, and his entire body seemed to relax. Even while at ease, he tended to stand with a slight stoop due to his war wound, but he did not do that now. He sighed heavily.

I stepped nearer to him, uncertain what was happening.

"Thank God!" His cry was so completely heartfelt that he instantly looked ashen-faced and turned away from me.

At that moment, I suddenly became filled with the thought—and the hope—that I knew what he was thinking, and offered him an inquisitive smile. "Why do you say that?"

"Because you are within my reach again," he explained, taking my hand. His voice trembled with emotion, which he was audibly struggling to hold in check. "Because I love you, Mary, as truly as ever a man loved a woman. Because this treasure, these riches, sealed my lips. Now that they are gone I can tell you I love you. That is why I say, 'Thank God.'"

"Then I say 'Thank God,' too." With that, he drew me into his arms, and I thought of the great fortune I had gained by the loss of that treasure.

16 July—I had to break off my writing last night, as recalling these events quite whipped me into a reverie. When I think how level-headed and pragmatic I used to be, such gaiety seems all the sillier. The Mary Morstan of six months ago would think me a strange regression to a fancy-taking juvenile. But I do not care for the views of that younger person, because I know that I am wiser for it.

Holmes brought the 'Sign of the Four' investigations to a conclusion last week. As he was putting the finishing touches on the case, he had less use of assistance. Consequently, I saw more of James, and we began to plan our happy day. The other day, on a whim, I had purchased a rather handsome picture of that esteemed veteran of the Crimean War, General Gordon. I had a feeling that, as an old campaigner and a keen military enthusiast, he would appreciate it. To my delight, he was very grateful and has set about getting it framed.

"It shall perfectly complement this one I have of Henry Ward Beecher, I think."

I must confess I did not quite see how the two pictures complemented each other, and James's desire to hang framed likenesses of them in our house seemed a touch eccentric. But so enthused was he at the concept that I did not chide him.

Tonight he is formally announcing his intentions to Holmes. "I shall have to broach the subject of departing from Holmes's side very carefully," he warned me, adding vaguely and darkly, "It could unbalance him quite considerably."

I teased him that he seemed more nervous about this aspect than about asking me for my hand.

In his absence, I invited my dear friend Kate Whitney to tea. Her husband Isa was out of town for the night, and she had not had the opportunity to congratulate me. I duly told her all about my dear James. I suspect I had begun to bore her, I was so besotted with him.

"He may have only his modest army pension and his practice, but we shall be quite happy. James does worry far too much."

"Forgive me," Kate asked, "who is James? I thought the gentleman was John Watson."

"Oh, I call him James. That is the name we have settled on for him."

"Mary, I am confused. Is his name James or John?"

"I had initially called him John, but he confessed that the name had bad associations for him."

"He didn't like his own name?"

"Oh, it is all his family, Kate. That family holds few happy memories for him. Just before I met him, his elder brother Henry died. It was a long and drawn-out affair, as the poor man had lapsed into alcoholism. It was the shame of his family."

Lest the reader think it indiscreet of me to discuss this with Kate, I should explain that shortly after we met, she had taken me into her confidence about some of her own troubles. Isa, you see, had his share of addictions. He fancied himself a poet, and at college had become so impressed with those writings of Thomas De Quincey that he became an opium addict. It was in fact, an episode relating to opium that had caused his hospitalization in July, when I first consulted Holmes.

Anyway, I continued relating our conversation to Kate.

" 'But you see, Mary,' James said to me, 'It was Henry who primarily called me John. After that, when I joined in the army, I tended to be addressed by my surname, and as Holmes has some of the vestigial mannerisms of a public schoolboy he has done the same. Therefore, I have not been called by my Christian name since my brother. Thinking about him …' And at this point he lost his composure. It is another reason we are so admirably suited to one another. We are both well acquainted with family tragedy. There is such sadness in him, Kate, and I believe I can help him overcome this."

"So how did you settle on James?"

"Well, I asked him what his middle initial stood for. 'Hamish,' he replied. 'And in truth I like that name even less than John.'

" 'Well, Hamish is the Scottish form of 'James', is it not? Perhaps that would be a suitable name?' And he agreed. This inconsequential conversation greatly lifted our spirits, and he much prefers having a name only I address him by. A pet name, I suppose."

"What's wrong with the name Hamish?" Kate asked.

"He considers it a pretension of his parents. There is some Scottish blood with the Watsons, and the Scots can be so ferocious about preserving their culture. But any schoolboy will prefer a simple English name that the class bullies won't mock."

"I wonder what schoolboys thought of a name like 'Sherlock Holmes'?" Kate asked with a smirk.

"As far as I understand, Holmes was tutored at home," I replied. "Perhaps that was why."

29 July—A few days have passed without incident. Preparations continue for our wedding, of course, though I grow somewhat impatient that the event itself is still entirely hypothetical. The date has changed a few times, as James has been so preoccupied with cases. It has been a matter of some consternation among my friends, in fact, who regularly tease me about the fact.

We have at least a church in mind: St. Giles's Cathedral in Camberwell. Mrs. Forrester saw to that, as a regular parishioner there. James and I are not particularly adamant churchgoers—I will attend with Mrs. Forrester from time to time, and James is often too occupied with various professional duties—so it was a selection made as a matter of convenience as much as anything else.

In the light of some of the cases he mentions, I do sometimes wonder if he is making excuses. For example, as soon as London was abuzz with stories of the favourite horse in the Wessex Cup vanishing, the next thing I knew he and Holmes were off to King's Pyland to find him. By this point I was all too familiar with my fiancé's penchant for gambling—some weeks it can claim up to half his wound pension—and so was mildly concerned. It was only on his assurance that Holmes would be accompanying him—and that he still, for James's own security, kept his chequebook locked in his desk—that I did not object to the trip.

Both men returned from the country in exceedingly good spirits. Holmes mentioned with a twinkle that he had stood to win on the resulting race.

"Such a breach of your professional ethics, Mr. Holmes," I chided him.

"You forget, Miss Morstan, that we detectives have none." He glanced sideways at James. "Unlike doctors, for example—yet you might be surprised how many reprobates our trigger-happy mutual acquaintance has maimed in the course of our adventures. As would the Royal College of Surgeons, I'd wager."

30 July—The trivial conversation yesterday, and James's buoyant spirits from his investigations, reminded me of my convictions about his general lifestyle. It is something I have vowed to adjust to, though I cannot imagine it will be a simple matter. He is again absent, and I have every reason to believe that this will be a regular state of affairs.

Mrs. Forrester insists that I should take a firmer line in this regard. However, she fails to appreciate that this is not James's wish but mine. James had fully intended to cease assisting Holmes at the conclusion of the 'Sign of the

Four' mystery, and indeed said as much to him when he told his friend of our engagement.

"Why on earth did you do that?" I demanded of him.

"For the simple reason that it is my intention!" he hotly replied.

"I'm sure you must have upset Mr. Holmes terribly."

"The kind of work involved in Holmes's cases is not fit to be carried out by a married man. There is no great shakes in risking life and limb as a bachelor, but my obligations and responsibilities to you, my dear Mary, must outweigh my friendship."

"I wouldn't allow it."

James grew apoplectic at my stubbornness, and demanded that I explain myself.

"Knowing both of you from our recent experiences, I can say that without you by his side, Mr. Holmes will take foolish risks and subject himself without thought to appalling dangers. The man has no clue how fast and loose he plays with his mortality. Think how close to death you came in the pursuit of the *Aurora* on the Thames."

"Yes, but it always seems like *me* who gets the poison darts," he commented ruefully.

"Only because of your protective instincts towards him. Were he on his own, or worse, aided by one of those bungling police officers like Athelney Jones or that

Lestrange[2] person, he would be in far greater peril. I'm surprised that someone with your keen observational skills fails to see how crucial you are to his life."

"I'm certain you're exaggerating. For all these words, I think Holmes would get on perfectly well on his own."

"I say that this is nonsense. You are like another distinguished James—James Boswell. And were it not for his self-effacing stability, the genius of Dr. Samuel Johnson would be unsung."

James seemed quite taken with this comparison. But he remained unconvinced, and redirected the focus of his appeal to me.

"Does that not put an awful burden upon you, my dear? Am I not asking you to share a place in my affections and priorities with a friend, a burden no man should ask of his wife? In view of the demands this particular friend can exercise, am I not even asking for greater priorities, still greater leeway to be given? Any woman would be forgiven for taking a firm stand in such matters."

"He is your friend, for all his exasperation, for all the high maintenance he demands you expend upon him. And were it not for that friend, I would not have met you, and not be in a position to become the happiest woman in the world."

---

[2] This is presumably a reference to Inspector G. Lestrade, who assisted Holmes and Watson in several cases. Mary Morstan never met the inspector; hence, she recorded the name incorrectly here.

I think often of these words, since I have seen so little of James recently. I am glad that I said them, and it makes the wedding well worth any amount of delay.

2 August—The wedding shall finally go ahead! All day I have been flurrying with activity, ensuring that the Banns will be called for the next three Sundays, and everything else is prepared for it. After so long waiting, it seems such a strange contrast.

This came about as the result of yet another late appearance by James at the house. It had been swelteringly hot in London all day, and the house still sizzled at this late hour. Mrs. Forrester was home this time, and almost did not admit him. I suspect that she thought the weather had affected his senses. He assured her it was an urgent matter, and I came to explain that it was all right, and that she could leave us alone. Though Mrs. Forrester is by no means prudish, I did see her purse her lips primly as she departed. And I must give the dear lady credit. For seeing James there, his breathing heavy, his face flushed with the heat, his eyes suffused with a curious mania, I nearly believed he suffered from some brain fever.

I was glad we were alone when James told me what had prompted his visit. He told of a horrifying affair concerning a cardboard box.

"It contained something utterly repulsive, which I am sure you would prefer I not reveal. It is horrendous enough for me to know it."

"James, please don't omit any details. It is terribly condescending to me."

He took a deep breath, and indeed I noticed he was suppressing a shudder. "Very well, then. Remember that I warned you. The box had contained ... two severed human ears."

This mutilation was but the gory post-script to a slow and dispiriting degradation of a man's love into alcoholism and violent murder. A sailor, Jim Browner, had his wife Susan turned against him by his sister-in-law when he had rejected the latter's advances. The elder sister introduced Susan to another suitor, and being made a cuckold drove Jim back to drinking, from which he had abstained for many long years—and to violence, which his temper naturally tended him towards. He returned home early from one of his voyages and surprised the couple on a boat, horribly murdering them, cutting off their ears, and then sending them to the sister, Sarah, whose fault Browner considered the whole wretched saga[3].

Watson was moved to tears by relating this case, and I too was very shaken by the end of his account.

"Even Holmes, whom I never expected to have such preoccupations, did not suffer the events lightly. The

---

[3] Published as 'The Cardboard Box' in the *Strand Magazine*, January 1893. Interestingly, it was omitted from the collected *Memoirs of Sherlock Holmes* published in December 1893. The decision was Arthur Conan Doyle's, and though it is not mentioned in his autobiography *Memories and Adventures*, nor by any other Conan Doyle biographer, it seems likely he excluded it because of either its sensationalistic violence, or its subject matter of marital infidelity.

morbid conclusion of the affair had moved him to ask: 'What is the meaning of it, Watson? What purpose is served by this circle of misery and violence and fear? It must tend to some end, or else our universe is ruled by chance, which would be unthinkable. But what end? There is the great perennial problem to which human reason is as far from an answer as ever.'"

The thought of Holmes possessing such a sensitive soul was, I admit, a further shock and emotional jolt in this whole account. We both sat there in tears for some time, and James, his hand shaking, gripped my own.

"I sat there with Holmes for a while after this dismal conclusion to the business, and then suddenly was compelled to see you."

"Why, James? What about this business made you want to see me?"

"Faced with such abhorrent acts, and the desolate motives that prompt them, I can and must marry you, my love, the very first moment that I can. *This* is the purpose that I see, and in you, I see an ideal far outside that circle Holmes described. I must seize what happiness I can when such random horror seems to close in all around my life like an inescapable noose. My love, I am so very sorry for having delayed it so long, as though it was something unimportant. Nothing, I swear to you, could be farther from the truth."

As he bade me farewell, and we had composed ourselves somewhat, I was moved to ponder how high emotions had run in our courtship thus far. It is so comforting to hear James tell me of the depth of his feelings, and I reciprocate them unstintingly. I am so very eager for us to be married.

25 August—We are officially wedded. What an occasion it was! The peal of bells from St. Giles still echo in my head (in the happiest manner of course). The excessive heat that began the month had cooled to tolerable levels, and so the sun shone and it was a golden day in so many ways.

We had realized early on that, since we are both orphans, Holmes would be obliged to perform multiple duties. He served both as best man to James, and led me down the aisle. Both tasks, but especially the latter, he performed with less aplomb than I might have hoped. However, I should not carp, as it once again reinforced how this strange man is the closest to family that either of us have.

We intended to hold the wedding breakfast at a modest venue near St. Giles, but Holmes very kindly furnished us with rooms at Lancaster Gate. Though ferrying the guests from Camberwell to Hyde Park was somewhat cumbersome, the venue certainly made the occasion far grander than I could ever have imagined.

As we proceeded in the brougham to the wedding breakfast, I recalled when Holmes told me of the place a week earlier.

"I am not devoid of sentiment, no matter what Watson may think," he had said. "And earlier in the year when we investigated the circumstances surrounding Lord St. Simon's bigamy[4], I thought how charming his wedding sounded. By chance, Lord St. Simon's father, Lord Balmoral, is an old acquaintance of mine, from that affair and the Wessex Cup business of 'Silver Blaze', so it was simplicity itself to arrange it with him. Of course, his son's happy occasion was marred by the disappearance of the bride at the breakfast. This in turn led to quite a nasty scandal, much grieved in society circles—"

Sensing, I imagine, Holmes distorting this gesture into a penny-lecture about the woes of marriage, James interrupted him harshly. "Thank you for the consideration, Holmes. Why not bore Mary with that another time?"

"I would have thought this the perfect time, since your good selves are about to enter into that happy state, as some have called it." Holmes made it clear in his tone of voice that he would not have agreed with those people. He added, cattily, "I hope not lightly."

At this, James had asked that I leave the room, and I had heard some raised voices and even scuffling. It seems scarcely creditable, as I write it, that I describe the behaviour of two grown men.

Holmes's thinly-veiled hostility to our union had not abated, though I saw little of him between that occasion and this day. So, when the gentlemen only appeared fifteen minutes late, there was a slight worry. I told Mrs. Forrester I was surprised it had not been longer.

---

[4] Published as 'The Noble Bachelor' in the *Strand Magazine*, April 1892.

I did not doubt, though, that the absence was the result of mere wedding jitters. Their wedding attire was in some disarray, and though James was impeccably clad, Holmes was wearing some virtually destroyed tweeds and a ridiculous cloth cap. He remained firmly inscrutable about what had kept them so occupied.

"It was an unexpected delay, Miss Morstan," he stated primly. "If you believe that I would keep Watson from his wedding, you forget that I must fulfil any task I am assigned, and merely meeting expectations would not be satisfactory."

"I must find fault with your reasoning," I admitted. "Surely if you were to exceed expectations, would you not have conveyed dear Dr. Watson here early?"

He flashed me a simpering smile and insisted, "That would have been quite impossible under these special circumstances."

James glowered at him, and said little to him during the wedding breakfast.

I was gratified indeed that so many friends attended to share this great day. Mrs. Forrester was doubly excited at the opportunity to see Holmes again. She began her re-acquaintance embarrassingly enough, announcing with inappropriate cheer that Cecil had passed away since she last saw him.

"That is most unfortunate," he said insincerely.

I left before I heard her continue her advances on Holmes, so it was only later that I learned she had fabricated many implausible scenarios to try to pique his interest. She must have spent nearly half an hour speaking of nothing but suspicious people lingering outside her window late at night, murdered men collapsing through her door, impenetrable ciphers being mailed anonymously to her.

Needless to say, if I could see through these flimsy penny-dreadful scenarios, Holmes could. Later, he remarked ruefully to me, "Your guardian Mrs. Forrester has had so many suspicious deaths around her, I am considering passing her details on to the officials at Scotland Yard. No person could be coincidentally involved in so much intrigue." Seeing that for a moment I thought he was serious, he added lightly, "However, at the moment I was content to introduce her to their emissary here, Inspector Tobias Gregson."

I looked across, and saw that she had latched on to him quite enthusiastically.

"Who would have thought, among all your talents, that you would be so skilled a matchmaker, Mr. Holmes?"

James then dragged me away to introduce me to a middle-aged, ex-military man. He was thrilled to see the fellow. "Mary, this is Stamford. He was my old dresser, and it was he who first introduced me to Holmes when I was invalided from Afghanistan. What was it, six years ago?"

"Yes indeed, sir. And from what I've read in the papers, your partnership has been highly successful. I never hear from either of you anymore."

"Well, Stamford, you have my thanks as well then. For had you not introduced Holmes to Watson, Watson would never have met me."

"You have my thanks doubly then, old chap!" James laughed.

"Indeed, chance is a queer thing," Stamford observed.

"Perhaps you could assist Holmes now that Dr. Watson shall be looking after me," I suggested.

Once we had left Stamford among the other guests, James revealed that Holmes's friendship with him was mainly rooted in his suspicion that the dresser had criminal connections. "This is why we could never have many friends," he admitted. "I am hoping, my dear, that you might help me become a more sociable fellow."

A familiar voice sighed behind us. "And in the aid of this ambition, my dear Watson, you have chosen a bride who is an orphan with few friends? I see that your reason is as haphazard as ever."

There was some unspoken appeal behind Holmes's words, as though he was asking for forgiveness with these mocking words. He got no reply whatever from James, who did not even look at him and angrily brushed past.

"What is the meaning of this hostility, Mr. Holmes?" I asked him.

"Miss Morstan—forgive me, Mrs. Watson—I should not burden you with my own neuroses on such a day. Suffice to say, and please note that I would never say it to him, Watson is quite right to bear me such ill will. Not

48

only have I been insufferable about his decision to leave my company, but I involved him in near-fatal intrigue only last night."

It was peculiar that emotions had run so high among friends of the groom. By contrast, my own friends were unburdened by any intrigue. Many of them said nothing more complicated than "Congratulations".

That is not entirely true. Kate was also there, and I saw her husband Isa for the first time since their wedding last year. It was a pleasure to see her, but I got the impression there was some implicit tension between them. Isa spoke in terse, brusque statements, and had a distracted air throughout the conversation. James noticed this particularly, as he was keen to meet them for the first time, having known Isa's brother Elias.

"Elias Whitney, D.D., was it not? Principal of the Theological College of St. George's?"

"Yes, indeed."

"I was briefly acquainted with him many years ago. What has become of him?"

"A most untimely death, after a long illness."

"That is truly sad to hear. He was an exceedingly talented man."

"He was indeed, Doctor Watson. I am certain that I haven't quite lived up to his standards, as I'm sure my family will attest. If you'd excuse me?"

"Is anything the matter with him?" I asked Kate.

"I think he's still getting over his illness," she said, unconvincingly.

In addition to his temperament, the man also looked exceedingly unwell—a deathly pallor was in his face, and he had lost considerable weight since his wedding. This was underlined by the fact that he wore an old suit, his neck poking through its collar like a pencil. I can only assume it was for his health that they excused themselves so early.

I also spoke for some time with a Scotsman. From the accent, and also his general bearing (he too sported a fine moustache) I thought he might be some relation James had not told me about.

"Not a relative, a colleague," he said.

"Oh, another detective."

He chuckled. "No, a doctor."

However, the man was more interested in discussing mystery than medicine.

"I keep telling Watson that these detective stories will be a craze. All those old ghost stories, sensation yarns, they're a thing of the past. The one I've just written for the *Pall Mall Gazette* has been very successful. It's called *The Mystery of Cloomber*. It's laid something of a corner-stone for me to give up medicine for a literary career. Have you ever read 'The Gold Bug' or 'The Purloined Letter'? Edgar Allan Poe?"

I knew the name of Poe, but confessed that I had not read those stories.

"He was a brilliant writer, but even he didn't have the advantage of drawing on real cases, like Watson does. And then there's that Holmes character. The science of deduction, I tell you! It reminds me of my medical professor at Edinburgh, Joe Bell."

"You are a doctor as well?"

"I have a practice in Southsea, but I simply couldn't miss the wedding of my old friend Watson."

He was in fact, a colleague from several years ago by the name of Doctor Arthur Doyle. The name was somewhat familiar, and Dr. Doyle told me he had offered James some advice to begin his fledgling writing career.

"I've just finished reading Dr. Watson's notes on the Agra treasure case. *The Sign of the Five*, or whatever."

"Four, Doctor Doyle."

"Ah yes. Well, in that case, Doctor *Conan* Doyle if you don't mind."

"Touché."

"I probably lost count of them midway through Small's recollection. Although that was nothing compared to *A Study in Scarlet*. The poor fellow, Jefferson Hope, had died almost as soon as they caught him. So when I wrote it up I had to flesh out a lot of that second bit about the evil Mormons. Did Watson ever show you that one?"

"I have heard of it, but haven't had a chance to read it."

"If I could have something like that, it might really help make my name. While I finish my historical novels that is. I really have a feeling that the name Arthur Conan Doyle might have some lasting fame thanks to *Micah Clarke*."

51

James found me and guided me away from Dr. Doyle. "Now, now, no literary talk," he admonished the Scot. "Was he telling you all about Edgar Allan Poe?"

"Perhaps Mrs. Watson might be interested in sport? I once took the wicket of W.G. Grace you know."

I hope I have another opportunity to meet this Doyle person. Unfortunately, a wedding day is such a frantic occasion, one never has long enough to meet with everyone. Honestly, the doctor's animated discussion was something of an oasis amid all the oft-repeated marital pleasantries.

I was sorry as well, when I heard that Holmes had departed early. The last time I spoke to him, I offered my sincere thanks to him for all he had done for James and myself. I also expressed my disappointment that he did not appear to be enjoying the wedding. Most of the time he had spent lurking in various corners, an *eminence gris.*

"You must forgive me for that, my dear Mary. You must understand that I am somewhat out of my depth."

"I find it hard to believe that could ever happen to you, Mr. Holmes."

I could not tell whether there was sorrow or a sneer in Holmes's response: "This smiling and trivial world is not mine. These mirthful and content folk are not my kin. I am exceedingly glad this world exists, and it could be argued that my skills and powers are ultimately dedicated to its preservation. For my dear friend Watson if not for my own sake, I am glad you have found a place for him in it. But there is no such place for me; I naturally dwell in the shadows, as I always have. And to the shadows, I think, I must retreat, now alone."

That was the last I saw of Holmes that night. Later on, Mrs. Forrester mentioned to me that at some point before we spoke, a tall and thin, academic-looking gentleman entered and looked around the room. She thought that he could have been Mr. Holmes's brother.

"He handed a waiter a card, which the waiter then presented to Mr. Holmes. There was the strangest expression on the man's face, and when he received the card, he looked across at him. Though they stood with twenty yards between them and made no move to speak to one another, there was a palpable, unspoken animus."

It was, according to her, shortly after this strange encounter that Mr. Holmes hurriedly seized his cloth cap and departed. He was not seen again that night.

"What did Holmes say to you, my dear?" James asked me very late in the evening.

"I cannot remember," I lied. Considering my debt to Holmes, I could not betray his confidence, even though it seemed disloyal to James. And bearing in mind that James was being irritatingly coy about this argument, I somewhat spitefully felt I did not necessarily need to reveal everything to him simply because we were married.

I did try one last time to tease out some more details. I asked James about Holmes's sudden departure and what it might mean. "Could it be anything important?"

He would reveal nothing to me, however. Lest the reader think we concluded our wedding night ruminating on a third party, I hasten to add that after this moment we ceased all talk of Holmes and turned to thoughts more befitting a newlywed couple. But at this query, his face hardened.

"I will not think about it again," he said simply. "It's just you and me, dear."

3 September—Mercifully, we have been able to enjoy a restful and uninterrupted honeymoon in France. I have not concerned myself with updating this record, and instead basked in the luxury of my husband's company.

He has fulfilled my every expectation of manhood. I can truly say that I had never expected to know the love that I have found with James.

In addition to knowing James so wholly, I have been able, in his company, to shed many of my foolish freaks and inhibitions. Foreign shores had, to me, the undeniable charge of tragedy to them, as I had been uprooted to England at such an early age and my parents were both claimed by them. Even France held some of this curse to me, a fact that James found unaccountably inexplicable.

James is a seasoned traveller, and he has happily regaled me with some of his experiences. In addition to his army service in Afghanistan, he spent some time of his youth in Australia. He teased me at one point that, "I have had experience of women that extends over many nations and three separate continents."

"As many as that?" I responded coolly. "You are fortunate indeed that I have come along, that is far too much experience for one man."

Though I bristled, the fact that James is so utterly candid with me, I feel, bodes well for our future together. So many men in this overly mannered age are preoccupied with what others will think, and how their words and deeds will be judged.

It helped, I believe, the romantic tenor of our trip to spend it in Paris. If more people had the means to travel here, it would surely surpass Brighton as a destination for those in love. There is an odd erection underway in the Champs-de-Mars. They are preparing for the Paris Exhibition, which looks to be a sizable event next year. It is a lattice of corrugated steel, designed by a young engineer named Gustave Eiffel.

I doubt M. Eiffel would be thrilled at Parisians' reaction to this project. As we strolled nearby, passing citizens would stop to decry it, and observe what a terrible disgrace it was to have such an eyesore blotting the city skyline. They took special care to point out that we, as English people, should not judge the rest of the city by this standard. "*Quelle disgrâce!*" was a repeated exclamation.

"As far as I understand," James informed me, "they are quite particular about the height of their buildings in this city."

"It is a striking design."

"Perhaps when they cover up the steel scaffolding with something more attractive, it will look better. It is so typical of modern designers, sticking up bits of flotsam irrespective of how they fit in with their surroundings. You wouldn't see a fairground stuck next to the Houses of Parliament."

5 September—We have now travelled about in the French countryside. The weather has been charming, and it is refreshing indeed to escape the bustle of Paris.

We have been extremely active. Though I know his wound was giving him terrible trouble, James gamely agreed to do some cycling with me in Lyons. We have also done some sailing, and James fished without success. "It isn't really the line of country for it," was his excuse.

We discussed Holmes only once during this blissful time. I simply had to know the cause of the hostility on that day. "You treated Holmes atrociously, if I may say."

James's pleasant demeanour sunk, and he sulked in silence for some time. But I would not let the matter drop.

"Was it the business he called you away on the eve of the wedding?"

"No, no. That was not entirely his fault, more his brother's."

"I had not wanted to mention this, my love, as it concerns you to some extent."

I became somewhat icy at this prospect. I understood that Holmes was a proud and dedicated misogynist, and James had tried for some time to divine the cause of this dislike.

This specific incident was not about my gender *per se*, but about our wedding.

"He said quite simply that he could not congratulate me."

"Did he disapprove of me?" I asked, the trepidation audible in my voice.

"Oh, not at all. In fact, you will be pleased to hear, he described you as one of the most charming ladies he has met, a decided genius was the exact phrase he used." He paused. "An assessment I concur with, of course."

"As do I. With what, then, do you take issue?"

"He thinks that marriage is an irrational thing."

"Surely that is his prerogative," I opined.

"His last words were what I took exception to. I remarked on his lack of credit for solving the mystery of *The Sign of the Four*. I was blessed enough to come out of the business with a wife, Athelney Jones somehow received the official credit, but he came away with nothing. I meant it sincerely, but he twisted my words against me. For how did he respond? He rolled up his sleeve, gestured to a nearby vial, and said, 'For me, there still remains the cocaine-bottle.' After all the work I have done to wean him off this dreadful and debilitating addiction, and he returns to it on a stupid whim. Worse, the whim is merely to spite me."

"I suppose even a mind as formidable as Holmes's must have its weaknesses."

"It is because of that blasted formidable mind that the weakness is so acute. Is it worth it, I wonder? To have

57

such advanced powers that narcotics are a suitable recreation? His constant need for mental stimulation, and its lack between his cases, is what drives him to that deplorable dependency. It's a voracious, horrific ... hunger. He speaks to me of elevating reason, and then makes that decision. I wish I had told him at the time how disgusted I was with him."

My idle comments had unleashed a torrent in James, and though I felt it was healthy for him to expunge these contained thoughts, I did feel I should have chosen a better time.

"But the implication behind it was even clearer," he continued, now in a real frenzy. "That he was prepared to sink into oblivion itself in my absence. That I should hold myself responsible for the consequences."

"I am sure he will cope."

"Mary, you forget that I've seen this kind of behaviour before. Henry was exactly the same. It was a vile display, a performance designed to sadden those who loved him. There is the same streak of deplorable exhibitionism in Holmes."

"We shall soon return to London," I said uncertainly. "I'm sure Holmes has not done himself any harm in such a brief period of time."

"Well, I will be damned if I am forced to be his nursemaid for the rest of his life! Especially now that I have you."

10 September—We are now three days back in London, and still coming to terms with our new life.

James has quite a backlog of patients to see in his new Paddington practice. This was quite a devalued concern, owned by a formerly skilled practitioner named Mr. Farquhar. James noted with some chagrin that his renown was once considerable, but its decline has been equally lamentable. Quite simply, the gentleman grew too old and infirm to keep up his standards—James attributes a virulent affliction of St. Vitus's Dance to his decline in respect among his patients.

"That seems a trifle unfair for so distinguished a professional?" I protested.

"You would think so, Mary. But consider it this way. The public not unnaturally goes on the principle that he who would heal others must himself be whole, and looks askance at the curative powers of the man whose own case is beyond the reach of his drugs."

His return to the metropolis, though, has occasioned a heaviness of heart, and I know he thinks of Holmes. At the moment, though, he is too busy to afford such time as full reconciliation requires. Indeed, his fellow practitioner has taken advantage of James's new eagerness to prove himself, and has taken a couple of weeks of additional holiday, and anticipates another long absence in a couple of months. It is a strange thing, as James often describes himself as by nature quite lazy, but he has positively thrown himself into his additional obligations. I blush with modesty at the thought that I may have galvanized him somewhat (incidentally, this comment was not made by me, but a jest of Mrs. Forrester's when I described the situation to her).

16 September—I am still enjoying married life (it is only a week, I am aware, but I still glow with bliss at the thought of it, which I remain sanguine enough to know cannot last indefinitely). Perhaps, though, some aspects of my life remain unfinished. For instance, I have lacked stimulation from the outside world of late and have agreed with Mrs. Forrester to resume my post as a governess in a temporary capacity. Never one to miss an opportunity to tease me, she has suggested that my yearning for activity is merely an unconscious wish to have a child. Though I am aware that my twenty-seventh birthday is approaching, I feel I am not too old to put off motherhood just yet.

Though it is not my primary concern, the extra petty cash this will afford us will be welcome. The move into our own house has been more of a burden than James had expected. I did not realize how much Holmes contributed to the financial situation! And I have had to take rather a difficult line with James about the gambling—it was our first significant disagreement since we have been married. To his credit, James has so far been as good as his word.

Just at the moment, though, we have just a couple of impecunious months to endure. It is in the aid of overcoming these obligations that James is presently forced to take on a great deal more patients than is sensible.

He currently shares his practice with Doctor Jackson Anstruther, an elderly physician. When I first helped James move his equipment into the new place, the sweet old man remarked to me, "Mark my words, Mrs. Watson, I can look after young Watson for you. I shall be happy to offer any assistance he requires, though I have my suspicions the young whippersnapper will be too proud to ask for help outright."

I admitted this was a possibility. When he lived with Holmes, his nominal occupation was largely at his discretion, but now he is really having to throw himself into it full-time. Although he approached it at first with his usual gung-ho attitude, I believe it is beginning to take its toll on the dear man. Several times this week he has come home at all hours of the night and collapsed straight into bed. In some ways I feel he is less suited to this quotidian work than the devil-may-care adventuring that had become his mien.

He was not overly favourable to my resumption of my governess position. "My dear, I had hoped the extra work would amply provide for us both! Hence my all-hours operations."

"Oh, were I thinking of financial matters I would certainly not be working as a governess," I said. "It is a good thing to have a place to go, work to do. I enjoy that measure of independence."

"So long as you enjoy it, I am happy for you to continue. I just wanted to make sure that it was not a shortcoming on my part that compelled you to it."

"James, I have experienced no shortcomings from you."

18 September—The most peculiar thing happened today. At six in the evening, I received a telegram from James, urging me to stay inside and admit no visitors. This was easy for me to comply with, as I had no engagements that day, and no one called. An hour later, James hurried inside, bolted the door behind him, and peered out the window for a full minute. He then ran to the windows in the sitting room, and upstairs, and did the same thing.

"Is anything the matter?" I asked him.

He turned to me and gave me a passionate kiss. "Mary, thank God you have not been harmed!"

"What is it?" I asked.

He pulled me to the window and indicated across the street. It was unusually early for James to be home, and our street was positively thronging with vendors. I remember the catsmeat man had given me a particularly rough time when I had left for milk in the morning.

James indicated a man standing by a brazier across the road. He was clad in a tattered black pea-coat, a broad and pock-marked face, dark glasses, and had a highly dubious beard.

"That man has been following me all day."

"He is wearing a rather obvious disguise."

I did not think that this thought had occurred to James, but as he regarded the beard he saw my reasoning.

"Who do you think this fellow is?"

"I would be willing to bet it has something to do with Holmes. He's antagonized so many people in our cases, and of course, now that he is not around they are no doubt persecuting me."

"My dear, you are sounding a touch paranoid."

"Oh really? Did I ever tell you of Grimesby Roylott, who entered our rooms and bent a steel poker just as a show of strength? And he, a man of learning and a medical man, stooped to employing a trained snake to murder his daughters."

"But you told me that he was killed, by that very snake."

"I didn't mean it was literally him, I meant that is the sort of character Holmes and I dealt with as a matter of course. And for every one who did meet a grisly end or was incarcerated, there remain those who were released early or had confederates still at large."

"Very well." I moved to the door.

"Where do you think you're going?"

"To Baker Street. If this concerns Holmes, then he is surely the one to talk to about it."

"By no means! I am still—"

"Sore with him over what he said before our wedding? And you would risk your wife's life because of that spat?"

I duly shamed James, but by the time we finished talking the stranger had left his post. James agreed to visit Holmes after work tomorrow evening. But knowing how late he finishes, I have decided to pay him a visit during the day. He carries so much emotion, that I feel I would be a more sober intermediary.

20 September—James saw the stranger in the streets again Tuesday, Wednesday, and Thursday. Once, he told me, he ran out into the street to pursue the man from his office. He was in the middle of a consultation with a new patient, whom I doubt will pay him a return visit.

In view of this week-long persecution, today was a perfect day for a secret visit to Baker Street. James was called away early to attend to a patient in Harrow, so I could leave freely.

Though Holmes's rooms were a more familiar sight, that trepidation I felt in July instantly resurfaced. I was certain I saw that strange bearded ruffian on the street corner, but a second glance made me think I had imagined it. Behind the bay window I saw that familiar massive head staring down at the street. Again I thought of a hawk surveying his unknowing prey—I felt he could swoop down and pluck some unsuspecting London criminal standing next to me. There was something beatific about his motionless stance, but also pitiless and arrogant. I could see then the truth of his words at our wedding—how could such a man feel happy descending to the level of us mere mortals?

When I saw that he had seen me, I offered a cursory wave up at the window. He did not move.

Mrs. Hudson, the aged housekeeper of 221B, greeted me at the door. The intervening months had sadly soured her disposition. The courteous elderly lady was rather curt and sullen with me as she led me upstairs.

I could not begrudge her this. "Mr. Holmes has become perfectly impossible since ... since."

"I am sorry to hear that."

"Doctor Watson was such a steadying influence on Mr. Holmes. I do hope you won't stand between them, Mrs. Watson."

"Nothing could be farther from my intention, Mrs. Hudson. Indeed, I have come here to mend fences because my husband is ..."

She nodded. "I know how the pair of them can get with each other. Sometimes I wonder if they shouldn't have married each other." At the mention of this, I wondered if I did not prefer her when she was sullen.

She led me into the sitting room. In the course of a few months, its disarray had grown acutely morbid. The aroma of the room was a mixture of at least three different types of tobacco and cordite. The very air of the room was thick, smoky and stale, which was not helped by the drawn blinds. When we got married we had moved some of the furniture to our new house, and that empty space was now filled with all manner of ghastly curios. As well as reams and reams of papers, a harpoon covered with gore was stretched across the table. The correspondence was now affixed to the fireplace by a hefty jack-knife. Most disconcertingly, the letters 'V.R.' were carved with rows of bullets into one wall.

I indicated this last item to Mrs. Hudson, who shook her head. "What is the meaning of it?" I asked.

Mrs. Hudson peered at the wall with her lips pursed. "Victoria Regina, I think," she suggested acidly.

I refused to let her temper put me off. "I gathered that. I meant, what was the purpose of this unusual tribute to Her Majesty?"

"Some testing of bullet calibres, I shouldn't wonder. All I know is, five minutes before it started I was on the other side of that wall. No consideration."

"And this object?" I asked, indicating the harpoon.

"I can't clear anything away, he just gets even more impossible. Hasn't had a case in months either. If he wasn't so inhuman, I'd say he could fall apart at any moment. This is why—"

"Doctor Watson should be here?" I finished, a hint of testiness filling my voice. "I hoped I might intercede on his behalf to fill that rift. But where is Mr. Holmes?"

I crossed to the bay window, behind which I had seen him standing from the outside. I stepped closer and was aware of a presence on the other side of the drawn velvet curtains. Mrs. Hudson stayed firmly on the other side of the room, and I gave her a somewhat withering look as I approached the curtain.

"Mr. Holmes? It is Mary, Mary Watson."

I gave the curtain a firm pull back.

Though I should not have been surprised, the sight caused me to jump back in shock. Holmes stood there, unmoving. There was something waxy and unreal about his flesh, and his hair had the texture of a wig. Despite these clues, it is only when—against my better judgement, I add—I reached out and poked his shoulder that I realized the truth.

The ginger pressure of my finger caused Holmes to topple forward into the window. Mrs. Hudson, her curiosity overcoming her dread of the man, approached me in horror.

I again rose above the criticism inherent in her question, "What happened? What have you done?"

"I have knocked over a dummy of Mr. Holmes, Mrs. Hudson. Though I had no idea even he would be such an egotist as to fabricate a replica of himself."

I must note here that it was an extraordinarily lifelike construction. This you must believe, as otherwise to be taken in by such a ruse seems the hoariest of theatrical clichés. I was at that moment utterly exasperated with Holmes, and think I was justified in kicking the stupid dummy before I righted it.

I looked out upon the thoroughfare of Baker Street. This time I was not imagining. The ruffian was standing next to a shop window, and made en extravagant show of lighting a dilapidated clay pipe.

Without a word to Mrs. Hudson, who stood agape at my deportment, I ran as fast as I could downstairs and out the front door. Thankfully a carriage obscured my egress, giving me the opportunity to surprise the man when I crossed the street. He looked haplessly about him as I caught up with him and made to run away. But I was faster, and clamped a hand on his shoulder in desperation.

"Mr. Holmes," I said archly. The performance was not over, though, and he launched into some exaggerated wheezing. To keep in the spirit of this game—even though my patience for it was long exhausted—I added, "Mr. Holmes would like to see you."

We entered the rooms and I saw him transform himself. The removal of the beard and dark glasses did some of the work, but the most significant transformation was when he relaxed his muscles. Where once his cheeks puffed outwards and his forehead was corrugated with age-lines, now he reverted to his bony, ill-nourished face.

"Most impressive," I remarked.

"Evidently not," he sighed, "as you were able to see through it so easily. Watson was always fooled, as were a great many criminals, I might add."

"It was not the disguise I saw through, at least not solely."

"Come, come, Mrs. Watson, you need not mince your words with me."

"In the plainest speech possible then—I merely eliminated the impossible and knew that whatever remained, however unlikely, must be the truth." Holmes gave a deferential nod at the quotation. "Who was the most likely person to be following my dear husband?"

"Congratulations. Despite my years of expert tutelage, Watson has not learned as much as you grasp instinctively."

"As usual, you do him a disservice."

As he slipped the dressing gown from the dummy onto his own shoulders, I began to appreciate Mrs. Hudson's concern. He looked even more skeletal than normal, and his pallor was now of the grey, putty-like hue of a corpse.

"On the subject of disservices, if you wished to make peace with Dr. Watson, why on earth did you resort to this ludicrous parlour game? Why not have the decency to confront him honestly? You quite unsettled him, traipsing about after him in that get-up."

"Well, it was a matter of …" He slumped back in his chair, and swivelled it angrily towards the window so I could not see his expression. "By the way, I was most chagrined at the way you knocked over my dummy by the window. I'm worried about assassination attempts, you see, and—"

I would not be drawn by this, and so pressed Holmes. "It was a difficult matter to discuss, even with a friend so close," was his ultimate, testy statement. "How have you found him as a husband? Up to your expectations?"

"I love him very much."

"Hmph."

If I did not know Holmes better, I would have thought there was a hint of jealousy in his enquiries. Mrs. Hudson's odd remark had probably gotten me thinking along these lines.

"And it is for that reason that I am here. As I tried to insist to him when we married, I see that your presence in his life is at the very least as essential as mine."

"Now, Mrs. Watson, I hardly think—"

"Who is mincing words now? As I was about to say, I take no issue with that—that arrangement. I hope that you will consult with him on future cases."

"That is a very accommodating attitude, Mrs. Watson. I am obliged to you. And I cannot argue that his assistance would not go amiss ... if I only had work to occupy me. And if you will bring every detail of our conversation back to him, as I know you will, I hope you will mention this." He grabbed what I took to be his cocaine bottle and threw it down on the table. It was still full.

"I was under the impression that it was a weakness of yours—"

"As was I, and you may add—as I know you will be compelled to by your sentimental feminine concerns—that it was a similar weakness of sentiment that prevented me from yielding, in spite of the intellectual atrophy I now suffer from."

"For all your fine words, Mr. Holmes, there are times when you seem to be doing nothing more than beating your breast like a cave-man."

I spent quite some time with Holmes, so that by the time James arrived at Baker Street, he had ceased his hostilities. Shortly before that, he even said, "I am glad that

70

your marriage has not changed you. You impress me as no less admirable than when we first met."

This compliment was still hanging in the air as James entered, hurriedly. "Holmes, I came as quickly as I could—why Mary! What on earth are you doing here?"

"Mr. Holmes called for me," I explained. "It was about that boorish ruffian who was following you yesterday."

"Yes, I must apologize for, er, his behaviour."

"What did the fellow mean, Holmes?"

"He was looking for me, I'm afraid, and knowing that you had formerly assisted me, it was natural that he should follow you. He has, ah, assured me that he will be more candid in the future and not resort to such cheap melodrama."

"Seems an odd way to say it."

"He is an odd man." I rose and went to the door.

"Mary, perhaps while I am here I might as well—"

"My dear James, I shall wait for you at home."

"Ah yes, thank you, Mary."

"You have my thanks as well, my dear Mrs. Watson," Holmes added with an eagerness that did not become him.

22 September—As glad as I have been since my marriage, it is only now that it is unalloyed in its completeness. And as happy as James was, I can see his reconciliation with Holmes has healed him somewhat as well. He has come back from his labours with an added energy and *joie de vivre*, and I have insisted that he drop by Holmes's residence at least twice a week.

25 September—I got a rather startling reminder of James's resumed intimacy with Holmes this morning. For as I rose, I found the man sitting in our kitchen, tucking in to a boiled egg my housekeeper had provided him with. He seemed completely at home, sitting at the table in shirtsleeves and dressing gown, as he often did in the comfort of Baker Street.

"Mr. Holmes!" I exclaimed in unalloyed shock.

"Good morning, Mrs. Watson," he beamed. "Incidentally, I am sorry your housekeeper has not come to terms with the death of her husband and that she is currently looking for employment elsewhere."

"I am sure you would like me to ask you how on earth you come to know these things," I replied.

"Simplicity itself, when one considers that a three-minute egg has by its consistency clearly been ignored for at least five and a half minutes, and a several-year-old picture of the deceased man is affixed to the opposite wall at a sufficient height to distract her as she reached for the salt. The tear-stains on her apron added to this supposition. As she set down the plate, the mark of ink from the paper she had put down to prepare the aforementioned egg left the letters V, A, C, and A—most likely from 'Situations Vacant'. For the sake of the evidence provided, I would of course overlook her preparation of my breakfast with such poor hygiene. She is no doubt an excellent employee when her efficiency is not hampered by personal tragedy."

"I admit that is rather impressive," I conceded. Holmes let out a disgruntled snort. "I did not hear you come in last night."

"I burst in on Watson in the middle of his last pipe. He was kind enough to put me up in your spare room."

"I suppose I may infer that this is not a social call, and that you are about to embark on a case with my husband?"

"That is so. We shall be going down to Aldershott. It is another military matter, the supposed murder of Colonel Barclay of the Royal Mallows[5]. It bears some similarity to that matter that brought us into contact with you two months ago. Far more puzzling, though—it took place in a locked room." He cast a disdainful glance down at his pocket-watch. "Who knows if I will ever get to solve it though, sitting here waiting for the slow fellow to finally get himself together."

"James is a late riser."

"Oh, I have years of bitter experience to attest to that. He snores quite loudly too, as you've probably noticed."

Poor James entered at this point, fastening his collar and hurriedly pouring himself a cup of coffee. "Come Watson, you will have to limit your repast to this stray slice

---

[5] This case was published as 'The Crooked Man' in the *Strand Magazine*, July 1893.

of toast." He inelegantly dropped the remaining slice from the toast rack onto the nearby plate.

"Need I remind you, Holmes, that the reason I have slept so late is because you kept me up all hours of the night recounting the facts of this Barclay case? Which I had to write down for the purposes of the records ... I also had to make the arrangements with Jackson to cover my patients for the day."

"Yes, yes, yes. Watson, you are talking when you should be eating. We have less than an hour to make it down to Victoria to catch our train."

A matter of minutes later, the two gentlemen donned their hats and left me.

3 October—The housekeeper gave her notice today. James was shocked to hear of it, but I merely said that I had a feeling that she might.

28 December—In the interests of Christmas, I have subjected James to visiting my friends—which, I know, is a taxing gauntlet for a husband to run. I sensed a look of ennui beneath the bonhomie he unfailingly embodied at their idle—and no doubt to him, interchangeable—chatter.

Therefore, yesterday, I suggested that he call at Baker Street. It seemed some time in Holmes's company was just the thing to revive him. "Otherwise, your face might just set in that rictus grin I saw last night at the Huxtables'."

I was exceedingly happy to receive a telegram in the early evening, informing me that he and Holmes had to return a Christmas goose to its rightful owner. Having been out of the practice of Holmes's excesses, I thought this was some whimsical nonsense on his part. It was thus a double surprise when James did not return, instead sending another telegram this morning claiming that the trail of the goose had occupied them for most of the night, and it was better that he stay over at Baker Street so as to follow new developments early in the morning.

To my shame, I did come very close to suspecting some mendacity on James's part when he said that within the crop of the goose was the famously missing Blue Carbuncle.

"Knowing from those six pearls that you are an admirer of bonny trinkets, I received a special dispensation from Holmes to bring it home to you to have a look at."

"I do not believe it."

No sooner had my scepticism been stated than James made me feel doubly foolish by producing the great jewel from his breast. It did indeed make my pearls look like common paste. There was something hypnotic about the way the light reflected through it, coupled with its unusual colour of brilliant azure.

"I do hope you intend to return this to the Countess of Morcar," I warned.

James arched an eyebrow. "I am sorry that I ever doubted your motives in returning to work. You make such a natural governess. When you take that tone, I feel like a six-year-old caught scrumping. Although my headmaster was not nearly so fine-featured as you."

"What a relief to hear that."

"But yes, the Countess is calling on Holmes tomorrow morning. So we must not lose it. Nor can we keep it."

I held it up by the fireplace, and gazed on its radiant glow again. "Oh well."

"Believe me, I am doing you a favour. This jewel has attracted more than its fair share of tragedy in its long history. Theft and murder were never too much for the avaricious pirates who have coveted it. Even this case had an innocent labourer jailed for the theft, and the real thief was a pitiful wretch who was egged on to it by the wicked waiting-maid of the Countess. As a side note, I cannot say I would recommend staying at the Hotel Cosmopolitan if I were visiting London from abroad."

"What about this Countess? Has she led a tragic life? Surely not materially, if this is anything to go by?"

James cleared his throat with all the tact he could muster. "She's not very nice to know. I heard Holmes mumbling 'dragon-lady' to himself."

1889

In the summer of '89 ... I had returned to civil practice, and had finally abandoned Holmes in his Baker Street rooms, although I continually visited him, and occasionally even persuaded him to forego his Bohemian habits so far as to come and visit us.
— *'The Engineer's Thumb' (1892)*

5 January—I have spent the last week feeling quite ill. No doubt it is merely the bad weather and an inevitable counterweight from my busy schedule over Christmas. I haven't the strength to get out of bed today, so I will content myself with updating my journal.

Writing this down seems like carping, but I feel the worse for being alone. James left late last night, and forgot to leave a note for me. Our maid will also be away for the next two days, so I am quite alone in my illness.

I wonder whether it relates to a curious thing that James said the other day. From what I gathered, there is some particular anniversary in two days' time. Last night— when I was feeling perfectly fine—James spent dinner looking forward in the calendar to see what patients he could expect in the coming week. He fixed on January 7 and remarked gloomily, "The seventh. A whole year since … since Holmes mentioned him."

Who could this person be? Is there any significance to the date? I do know it is the day after Holmes's birthday. It does explain his fondness for quoting *Twelfth Night* above all other Shakespeare plays. When I am feeling better, I shall surreptitiously consult James's casebooks and get to the bottom of this.

It does rather irk me that James is so protective over his notes. As a governess I am naturally adept at editing and proofreading duties. One of the benefits of having no parents to rely on was that it compelled me, when I was younger, to take up clerical training. I am a competent typist. When I mooted the possibility, James firmly rejected it.

In fact, in the short time I have been married to him, I have seen James's temper become perfectly terrible at times. It always concerns matters related to Holmes. My typing suggestion, for instance, was impractical because of the sensitivity of some of the cases. That is all very well, but there is no need for him to berate me so for making a perfectly simple suggestion. Especially when I do so out of a desire to protect his interests, something that Conan Doyle is singularly uninterested in.

No doubt my illness is compelling me to these ruminations. Only a few days ago, on Christmas Day, I had no cares in the world and was enjoying the full festivity of the season. In previous years, I would sometimes get carried away with my life's problems around the Yuletide season. This year, for the first time, I felt the true spirit of this joyous season. With James at my side, there stirred deep in my breast an impression, a conviction even, that something wonderful was around the corner.

10 January—James returned today, and could not stop reproaching himself for his absence. From his examinations, it seems that I am with child.

Of course, I could not be more pleased! James also. It is so obvious to me that my extremities of emotion over the past couple of weeks were my intuition that this greatest of blessings had been bestowed upon me.

James could not stop chastising himself for his absence. "If anything had happened... any complication ... I would have felt so completely responsible." He became quite fraught with emotion, and I assured him that there was no need. My previous journal entry will attest that I did not quite feel this way the other day, but in this context, hopefully that was a forgivable lapse.

So full of remorse was James that he told me he has made arrangements with his neighbour-doctor, Jackson Anstruther, to take on some of his patients should any circumstances with me arise. As an older, solitary man, Doctor Anstruther was only too happy to oblige, and I am so glad that he has been so accommodating.

It is amusing how one's change in circumstances can so radically alter one's perception of unrelated events. Suddenly, every piece of news I hear seems to have some romantic dimension to it, no doubt a refraction or distortion of my approaching motherhood. I asked James to tell me of the case he was working on as a way of taking his mind away from endlessly chastising himself. It was, he told me, a political intrigue surrounding a woman with whom the King of Bohemia had an indelicate affair[6].

Not only had Holmes once again let the culprit—an adventuress from New Jersey named Irene Adler—evade justice, indeed it had seemed that she had outwitted him. Furthermore, though Holmes himself would never admit it, James was certain that he saw some stirrings of romance in Holmes's icy misogynist heart.

Could it be, that even that heartless thinking machine was capable of romantic feelings? Could one day a child of Holmes and Miss Adler be out in the yard playing with my future son or daughter?

Alas, the story ended with Miss Adler escaping the country, and Holmes had no way of keeping in contact with her. Since the case has resolved, he has not only ever referred to her as 'the Woman'; but—and this detail, I confess, brought a tear to my eye—he kept a photograph of her as a reminder.

I have every confidence that James will be a wonderful father. The timing is less than ideal, given his heavy schedule of late. I know he has been in touch with Conan Doyle about publication of more Sherlock Holmes stories, but the man has been frustratingly vague about it. As I have read over a few instalments of what James calls 'The Casebook of Sherlock Holmes', I can say that he has made procedural details that work as exciting adventures. I think many readers, myself included, would most definitely

---

[6] Published as 'A Scandal in Bohemia' in the *Strand Magazine*, July 1891.

welcome seeing this work in print. Though I may blush to see my own name mentioned, should he ever adapt 'The Sign of the Four'. Perhaps I'll be edited out.

2 February—I have not been out of the house recently. I think I am firmly adjusted to my pregnancy. With some sadness, I gave my notice to Mrs. Forrester.

"It scarcely seemed worthwhile to take me on again, since I am now leaving your service."

"Oh, don't be silly, my dear! I hope you remember that I shall be available for whatever assistance you need. Even though your dear Dr. Watson means well, if ever circumstances arise when you need someone and his attention is occupied…"

"Of course, Mrs. Forrester. I would always have considered you to rely on." Having said that, I wonder how quickly it will be before I need to make good on this promise. James has yet more patients to see and more investigations to make. The inactivity that had forced the detective to shadow after his friend seems likely to have ended for the time being.

10 March—My last social engagement for what will probably be quite a while was, unfortunately, a far from pleasant one. The Whitneys invited us over for dinner. James has always detected a certain tension with Isa, but has been willing to tolerate it due to my affection for Kate.

From the moment we entered, the evening was fraught. Kate was her usual ebullient self, but there was a touch of mania in her pleasant manners. It was quite clear to us that there had been some dreadful altercation shortly before we had arrived. As soon as she left the drawing room to get us a drink, James said as much to me.

It became a ghoulish inversion of a stage farce. Whenever we began to talk amongst ourselves, one or other of them, or a servant, would enter the room. Isa did not come down for nearly an hour after we arrived.

He looked so appalling as to make the unhealthy Holmes I had seen back in October look a fine figure of a man. His lips were a gash of scarlet, and similar red circles were etched around his eyes, which stared out with the haunted emptiness of a man possessed. His hair clung to his scalp, slick with dried sweat.

James embodied *politesse* as he made small talk with Isa. Even when the man is at his most concentrated and affable, James found little to talk to him about. Right now, though, he was distracted and restive, constantly looking to the corners of the room and shifting in his seat.

When Kate entered with our drinks, Isa fixed her with an expression simultaneously lewd and poisonous. "There is my dear muse," he said, though the compliment had no warmth. "What would I do without you my dear, my dear?"

Kate remained silent, and tried to change the subject to my child. Isa remained silent, but then let out a most inopportune ejaculation. "I know what Kate is thinking. I was never so fortunate as to father a child."

"I did not think that," Kate insisted. Her voice had a low, brow-beaten agitation to it.

"Why not be honest? Why can no one ever be honest? All the manners in the world, and nothing we say can ever describe how ... how unfailingly *wretched* everything is."

"Kate, is everything all right?" I whispered.

"And all that secrecy too!" he thundered. "Whispering secrets. Of course, I can't expect any different from you women. How would you know what anything was like? Eh? You haven't seen outside your parlours!"

James rose to his feet. "I think that you should moderate your tone."

"Jack and I know what it's like, see," he sneered. He stood toe to toe with James, and then slumped forward so that he was half-standing, half-leaning against him. James was positively boiling with rage as he continued his thoughts. "D'you know what civilization is? It's men in pits of vice, willing to gouge each other's eyes out for another dose. You should know, after all, I thought you'd gone to Afghanistan. It's bad enough here with all the Chinamen in Soho, I can't imagine what that lot of savages are like."

"When I was hit with a Jezail bullet," James said, "my life was saved by an Afghan. If that is how a savage behaves, I cannot imagine what one would call this disgrace. Your brother—"

"Not my brother!" he wailed. "Not him again! How often do I have to be compared to him, to all the other blasted Whitneys... the apple has fallen far from the tree,

83

how I tire of hearing it said. No one ever asked me if I wanted to be an apple on that tree in the first place, as I recall."

"You shame his memory, speaking of him like that, you ... you sot!"

James was quite literally fuming with anger by the time he roared these words. It seemed to awaken some dim pride in Isa. With little grace, he lashed out at James, but his energy dissipated as quickly as it reared itself. He was as limp as a rag when James and the servant carried him to bed.

"I am sorry about all this," Kate said, visibly holding back tears. "Perhaps we can do it again some time, when Isa ... when Isa is feeling better. I can't think of an explanation. I suppose it must be overwork."

"Would you like to tell us about it?" I asked again.

"Goodnight, Mary. Goodnight, Doctor Watson."

"Kate," James insisted. "I will not leave this house unless I am certain that you will not be harmed by this person."

"No, Isa, has never harmed me," she said. "Not physically, anyway. It is only cruelty and bullying of the mind he inflicts on me."

Realizing neither of us could do any more, we made to depart. James insisted on giving Isa a hypnotic to help him sleep—and preserve Kate from any molestation.

16 March—Kate called on me today, even more distressed than she was the previous weekend. "I was so dreadfully embarrassed by Isa's conduct, I simply had to speak with you about him."

I insisted on pouring her a glass of wine, so fragile she seemed. "It is opium," she ultimately told me.

"My God, Kate. I am so sorry."

James had his theories on the subject. Isa's specific comment about 'Chinamen in Soho' indicated something of this nature.

"He had first seized on the poison in his college days, long before I had met him. His scholarship had taken him to the writings of Thomas De Quincey, I think the fellow's name was. *Confessions of an English Opium-Eater* was a tome he consulted very freely. From there, he was seized by a … freak about the subject. He began by putting laudanum into his tobacco."

"When did you learn of this?"

"He wrote down his dreams in this state, just as De Quincey had. He showed it to me to try to make me understand why he so compulsively continued his horrible self-mutilation. That was a few years ago, and he had tried to swear it off. Then, he cared for me enough to put my needs above his cravings. It seemed for a while that he was successful, but lately he has been drawn right back into its wretched pull."

"And what happens when he is in the throes of his opium?"

"The fits that seize him are truly terrifying. He will vanish without trace, and return late at night, a changed man." She sipped her wine and shuddered. "Drastically changed."

"Has this vile behaviour caused him to harm you? Mark my words, Kate, James could—"

"No!" she cried in some horror. "Don't say that James would hurt him. He is already hurt enough by this crippling vice."

"I was going to say that James could help him overcome it. He would be happy to, if he were certain it would vouchsafe your well-being. And as long as no harm has come to you."

"You saw him the other night. It has reduced him to such a feeble condition that he could not inflict any harm on me if he wanted to." She paused, and took a long sip of her wine. "No physical harm, anyway. It manifests itself mainly in cruelty, rages. I have tried so hard to make him happy, but he has a wildness to him. And of course, we cannot seem to have children. Sometimes I think I may have driven him to it, that there was something about me..." She broke into weeping at this stage, and I took my old school friend in my arms.

"Kate, you must not blame yourself for this. I am aware that you love Isa, but he walked down this road himself. I know you too well to think that anything you could have done could bring him to this state."

We spoke late into the night. When we left, though I know Kate was still racked with worry over her husband, she was calmer. I promised I would tell James and we would help her overcome this.

18 March—I spoke with James about Kate and Isa, and he said he would help if he could. "It is somewhat outside my field," he admitted sadly. "A great deal depends on the willpower of the addict. And—believe me when I say that I have a heavy heart at these words—I doubt Isa has that fortitude. Kate deserves far better."

"I cannot help but agree. Is there anything you can do though? Any hint of experience from dealing with Holmes?"

"It all depends on the case. For Holmes, the dependency was a weakness, but one he was able to hold remarkably in check. That mind, Mary—that marvellous brain of his. Though it was the cause of the affliction, it at least prevented him from succumbing to the full, pathetic decline that Isa so fully embodies."

As far as I knew, the other reason Holmes had given up his cocaine—the 'weakness' of sentiment that he spitefully told me about—remained unsaid to James, who attributed it entirely to his medical skill. For the sake of preserving his high opinion of his work, and also for respecting Holmes's wish that his dear Watson not know his occasional humanity—I concealed this fact from him.

I know a wife should ideally conceal nothing from her husband, but given the unusual circumstances of his relationship with Holmes, I felt I was justified. It gave me pause though. If it was Holmes's humanity and affection for others that had conquered his dark side, surely Isa would be capable of a similar change of heart?

"Damn the man," I finally declared.

James was shocked at my tone. "Kate loves him very much," he said.

"Exactly. So I damn him again. You know Kate now, James. Would you not say that she was a fine, intelligent young lady?"

"Certainly I would."

"By what right, then, does this spineless, feckless Isa drive her to despair, for the sake of his own compulsion to self-harm?"

"Perhaps she considers it worthwhile, if she loves him."

"Is that right, though, James? Should someone be so dependent on one so unworthy, that they would put that person's feelings above her own happiness?"

"You allow me to spend time with Holmes. Some might argue that was a more reckless habit than opium addiction."

James's levity broke my introspection, and I tried to put it out of my mind. After all, there is nothing I can say or do to induce Kate to leave her husband's side. It must be her decision alone.

4 June—Sometimes I feel rather guilty at the way that I can send James off packing. However, he has been rather worn down of late, and so when a telegram arrived during our breakfast this morning, I spied an opportunity to improve his spirits.

HAVE YOU A COUPLE OF DAYS TO SPARE? HAVE JUST BEEN WIRED FOR FROM THE WEST OF ENGLAND IN CONNECTION WITH THE BOSCOMBE VALLEY TRAGEDY. SHALL BE GLAD IF YOU WILL COME WITH ME. AIR AND SCENERY PERFECT. LEAVE PADDINGTON BY THE 11:15.

I could see poor James positively chomping at the bit with curiosity, yet he regarded the telegram with a frown. He looked up and down, back and forth at the object all through his breakfast.

Finally, I asked, "What do you say, dear? Will you go?"

He hummed and hawed, and finally admitted, "I really don't know what to say. I have a fairly long list at the moment."

I saw his heart was really in the prospect of this trip to the west. "Oh, Anstruther would do your work for you. You have been looking a little pale lately. I think that the change would do you good, and you are always so interested in Sherlock Holmes's cases."

"I should be ungrateful if I were not, seeing what I gained from one of them," he answered, clasping my hand in his as he said so. Immediately, though, he withdrew it and rose to his feet, combining the action with a long swig of his tea in a sudden flurry of excited activity. "But if I am to go I must pack at once, for I have only half an hour."

He came down a few minutes later, hat in hand, extolling the virtues of his days as a traveller in Afghanistan. "I'd like to see a chap who can pack a valise that quickly and precisely."

"Happy travels," I said as I kissed him farewell. It seems characteristically morbid to write such sentiments down, but there is a curious paradox in the fact that the worse the horrible event that draws Holmes and Watson into a case, the more invigorating both men find its stimulation. With that being the case, I have no doubt that a bit of Boscombe Valley tragedy is exactly the thing to restore the good doctor's rude health[7].

19 June—The Whitneys' story, which for so long lay ominously unresolved, was unexpectedly brought up to date this evening. James was rubbing his eyes and contemplating an early night, while I was in the middle of some needlework, when the bell rang. I had been keenly anticipating a quiet night in with James, and so did not disguise my disappointment.

"A patient!" I sighed. "You'll have to go out."

He merely groaned in reply. Shortly thereafter Kate entered, her face obscured in a black veil and her clothes similarly dark. With the weather as pleasant as it had been lately, I knew this apparel was an ill portent.

She had barely emitted, "You will excuse my calling so late," before her composure completely

---

[7] This was published under the title 'The Boscombe Valley Mystery' in the *Strand Magazine*, October 1891.

collapsed. She collapsed in my arms, and sobbed uncontrollably for a time. "Oh! I'm in such trouble! I do so want a little help."

We had both long anticipated this call from Kate. However, as James had said after that dreadful evening in March, "I cannot guess the reason for her trouble, I can guess the man responsible. But what can we do if she doesn't come to us?" James was always so sweet in his concern for those in need. Whereas Holmes viewed the tapestry of turmoil in London society as a magnified, perpetually extended laboratory experiment, my dear husband saw it almost as a crusade.

Now that this long-awaited moment had come upon us, I felt I must try to buoy Kate's spirits. James teased me that I was becoming positively maternal in my pregnant state, and that folk in grief sensed the fact, coming to me like "birds to a lighthouse".

"Now, you must have some wine and water, and sit here comfortably and tell us all about it. Or should you rather that I sent James off to bed?"

Though I could see James would have welcomed that, he was equally prepared to remain by my side. Kate emphatically replied, "Oh, no, no. I want the doctor's advice and help too. It's about Isa."

James pursed his lips as he poured us the refreshment, and Kate explained: "He has not been home for two days. I am so frightened about him!"

We both gave her as much assurance as we could, and I tried to focus on practical matters. "Do you know where he might be? Perhaps James might be able to find him for you."

"I would be glad to," James immediately interjected.

"After last night passed without him returning, I was sick with worry and simply had to know for my own sake. So, I contacted a friend of Isa's, who reluctantly told me that he visited an opium den in London's furthest east corner. Its name is the Bar of Gold, in Upper Swandam Lane."

James was in firm 'Dr. Watson' mode, and gleefully took note of all she said and approvingly murmured, "Mm, that is some positive information."

"But is it, James?" she asked. "What could I possibly do? I haven't the strength to wander into that benighted part of London to extract my husband. The very thought of it drives me even further to despair."

This was James's final call to arms. He rose to his feet. "There is no question of you going alone, Kate. I shall accompany you." He paused a moment, and corrected himself. "Indeed, I shall go on my own. There is, when you consider it, absolutely no need for you to subject yourself to such insalubrious conditions. I am used to them ... er, from my time with Sherlock Holmes that is."

"Oh, if only Mister Holmes were here to help," Kate mused.

"He's heavily involved with some investigation or other at the moment, as far as I remember. I've fallen behind on his activities," James mumbled apologetically. It was always his way that when a friend would speak admiringly of Sherlock Holmes, he would become bashful and contrite about his own talents.

"Believe me, Kate, James is far more reliable than Sherlock Holmes," I insisted. With that, James grabbed his hat and stick—and even brought his revolver for safety's sake. He instructed that he would send Isa home within two hours.

I decided I should wait up with Kate. Though she was calmer, now she expressed some concern over James.

"Sending him off like that … oh, what have I done? Not only for his sake, Mary, but for yours!"

She had clearly not seen the ecstatic gleam in James's eyes as he prepared to depart. "I assure you, Kate, that it is exactly what James lives for."

Later—This night has turned me quite upset, though not for the reasons I expected. On the bright side, James was as good as his word. Within two hours, a carriage arrived. I was highly dismayed, however, to see that it only contained Isa.

He was a different man than the one who had berated and troubled us these last few months. He was piteously doubled over, cringed as he grabbed Kate in his arms, and shed tears no less genuine than hers a few hours ago.

"And it's all thanks to your husband, Mrs. Watson!" he declared. "There I was, in the hollow bliss of my opium reverie. What I thought were a few hours had passed. Then he appears out of that wretched darkness and tells me that, no, eight-and-forty hours I have left my dear wife's side. 'Your wife has been waiting two days for you. You should be ashamed at yourself!'

"Mary, please accept my profoundest apologies for my behaviour when we invited you over. Both to you and your husband. He is such a thoroughly decent man. I wish I could be such a man."

"I know you can be, Isa," Kate declared. "Let us go home."

"Before you depart," I interrupted, "where is that thoroughly decent husband of mine?"

"Oh, yes, all he asked—all, mind you, in exchange for which he paid my bills at the wretched Bar of Gold and this cab here—was that I deliver this note to you."

I bade them farewell and returned inside. My uneasy temper now became somewhat furious, I admit:

My dearest Mary,

It is the most remarkable occurrence. As I was extracting Mr. Whitney from the Bar of Gold, who should I happen upon but Holmes! He has asked that I assist him in a curious affair of a missing man, Neville St. Clair. The trail has led to this den of iniquity, and he needs my help following it further. I doubt I shall return home tonight.

94

It is, as you know, difficult to refuse any of Sherlock Holmes's requests.

Thank you, my love, for your patience, now and always.

Love,

James

This left me quite agitated! Indeed, only now that I put pen to paper can I bring down the anger I was gripped with at reading this missive.

First of all, Holmes has apparently traded one vice for another. All that talk of having given up cocaine merely concealed the truth. And if this is part of some investigation, Lord only knows what new depths of depravity he is leading my dear James into. I know crime and murder cannot take place in daylight and respectable drawing rooms, and I well remember my vow to not interfere in their friendship—but this seems so deliberately testing! And James's blithe acceptance irritates me even more!

And I was not solely thinking of myself, but of the resolution to this initial mystery. James was so distracted with Holmes's investigations that he happily sent Isa home unsupervised! The danger this may have caused Kate! The danger it may have caused *me*! No, there will be harsh words when James does return.

20 June—James did not return until late this afternoon. I had spent the entire day boiling in anger, but he was utterly oblivious. For as usual when he returned from an outing with Holmes, he was filled with childish enthusiasm for ever grisly detail of the freshly solved mystery[8].

He had just concluded telling me of how Mrs. St. Clair's husband Neville had disguised himself as a beggar, because he could gain a greater living from coins dropped in his hat at Shakespeare recitations than many other types of labour. His wife accidentally spied him in the vicinity of Swandam Lane, and his attempts to cover his tracks caused her to believe he had been murdered by the very beggar that he was, in fact, impersonating.

It was, in truth, a very interesting story, but I could not concentrate on its details. In fact, I interrupted him with a cry of the strongest disapprobation.

"My dear Mary, whatever is the matter?"

"James, you behaved thoughtlessly last night! As it happened, Isa was contrition itself when he returned, but I strongly suspect that you had forgotten all about him, about Kate, about *me*, as soon as Holmes seized you into this St. Clair business!"

He was taken aback by my rebuke. I was somewhat exhausted from the invective too, now that I had said it. I would not take back one word of it, however, because I maintained that his lack of thought had brought a needless

---

[8] This case was published under the title 'The Man With the Twisted Lip', in the *Strand Magazine*, December 1891.

jeopardy on ourselves and Kate—not to mention our unborn child.

"On top of all this," I was compelled to add, "Mr. Holmes clearly has a new and even less savoury drug habit! All your fine words about his intellectual resistance to the lure of drugs—we now see how true they were!"

"Mary, take me to task by all means, but there you are mistaken. Holmes was in disguise. He had taken on the appearance of an old wretched opium addict to follow the St. Clair case the better. In fact he was in quite robust condition. When we stayed over at Mrs. St. Clair's house—"

"You did what?"

It took James a moment, and then he chuckled smugly at my interpretation. "Ah, not … there was no impropriety. We were forced to bed down there for the night as it was nearer the scene of the crime, as it were. It was easier for us to follow the trail from there."

"Is Holmes … interested in any way in Mrs. St. Clair?"

"My dear Mary, he has found her husband. His interest is only as a client. You really do not know him well."

"So I am learning."

James had patients to see in the afternoon, and so has left me alone. It was probably the wisest thing he had done that day.

97

21 June—Tensions have eased, as James quite sensibly realized he was at fault.

"There is no excusing my actions. I sometimes forget my responsibilities where Holmes is concerned."

"Though I think you're right, I possibly overreacted slightly as well. You did at least find Isa as you said you would. But you could see how I might feel slightly abandoned when my husband drops an opium addict on my doorstep without bothering to come back himself."

"Quite, Mary. I was prepared to cut Holmes loose when we married, something that would have caused me great pain. So relieved was I that such a measure was not necessary, I may have come to take for granted your extraordinary understanding and generosity in allowing me to remain by his side."

"And you must in turn forgive me. It is sometimes galling having to share my husband, especially with another man."

"Count yourself lucky that I am not having affairs into the bargain," he joked.

"I think it would be simpler if you did," I suggested. "At least I would then know where I stood."

"I am aware that you may not feel like going away, but what would you say to a weekend in Brighton? I have made all the arrangements, and what few patients I have scheduled I could easily make arrangements to see next week."

So this afternoon, I write this entry bound south. It is an ideal summer weekend, and I am still mobile enough to enjoy the sea air.

23 June—Any lingering anger at James's conduct the other day was permanently banished when we were faced with a curious echo of the business with Holmes after our wedding. Several times over the course of the day James had remarked that an elderly dowager had sat, unmoving, in the lobby of our hotel. In the afternoon, he had seen this ominous lady out on the terrace enjoying an aperitif,

She looked most out of place amid the gay surroundings of Brighton. She was wearing heavy black, including long black gloves covering her hands, and her cheeks sagged in flaps around her face, which gave her a permanent aura of sadness. Her eyes were obscured by dark glasses, and she looked weighed down by her cumbersome layers.

As we returned from the beach to enjoy an early evening drink, James saw her again. I confess that up to this point I had barely noticed her.

"She is still there! She has been sitting on that terrace for nearly three hours. Not doing anything, just staring ahead and drinking that *crème de menthe.*"

"Is that so?" I was feeling slightly drained from spending so long in the sun, and so was not terribly interested in his conversation just now.

"I'm going to put this to an end once and for all." He left my side and strode to the terrace. "All right, Holmes, enough is enough. I cannot allow you to follow us around all the time like this!"

The dowager looked up at him in confusion and mumbled some words. She appeared to be hard of hearing, and was struggling to raise a trumpet to her ear. James rolled his eyes at this display of exaggerated feebleness.

"Now come off it Holmes! This is beyond a joke!"

He then reached forward and pulled off her glasses. She did not react, so he began pulling on her cheeks.

A few minutes later he returned to my side and suggested we go elsewhere for our drink. "I have made the most enormous mistake."

Thankfully the dowager was so old, and according to the hotel staff of somewhat weakened faculties, that she barely noticed this extraordinary behaviour. The rest of our time passed without further intrigue, though as a lover of juvenile humour, I laughed about James's misapprehension, and his continuing embarrassment over it, at considerable length.

25 August—Our first anniversary. We had no particularly grand plans, but James took it upon himself to surprise me with a pheasant that he prepared himself. Life with James is a constant reminder of good fortune, but on this night in particular I feel that I glow with reverie.

And to think that in a short while we shall both be parents! I am ecstatic, and I know that James will be a wonderful father to our forthcoming son or daughter.

3 September—A further burden, but one of the most exciting kind, came from that colleague Dr. Doyle. He came to town yesterday and took us out to dinner at Simpson's in the Strand. I saw James look over his shoulder a couple of times as we entered.

"Not Holmes, surely," I scolded him.

"It's just that it was one of our spots to dine, when we were on a case."

By this point, I knew that James's preoccupation with Holmes needed to be resolved, as he was becoming more obsessed with him in his absence than when they roomed together. "Please, James. Let us put Sherlock Holmes to one side this evening and instead have a pleasant time with Dr. Doyle."

"My dear, it's Doctor *Conan* Doyle. He's quite particular about that."

Having said all that, you may imagine what my reaction was when the first words to come from Doyle's mouth were "Sherlock Holmes"!

"I hadn't expected it either," he admitted. "But it's been so extraordinary. First *Study in Scarlet* got printed in book form, then *Micah Clarke* was released and received favourable reviews. Then one evening I was asked to dine with an American agent, James Marshall Stoddart. He was looking for talent for a new magazine called *Lippincott's*. I had dinner with him at the Langham Hotel. It was a truly golden evening, I must say—there was Mr. Stoddart, T.P. Gill … oh, and this other chap. A most extraordinary fellow, name of Oscar Wilde. You may have heard of him."

"Arthur, you can be the most appalling name-dropper," James declared through gritted teeth. "We all know who Oscar Wilde is!"

"Fair enough," Doyle replied. "But Wilde, what a prodigious mind. I don't know how, but he seems to have read just about anything I could mention. He had even read *Micah Clarke* and told me how enjoyable he had found it."

"I've heard Mr. Wilde is a voracious reader."

"Anyway, I recalled that you had this *Sign of the Six* story—"

"*Sign of Four*," James corrected.

"Yes, yes. That one—so if you can get me that manuscript, the deal is all done. Even better terms than *Study in Scarlet*."

He confessed, "I don't understand it, *Beeton's* paid me £24 for that, but I would have happily accepted two quid for *Micah Clarke*."

"Perhaps Sherlock Holmes will one day be even better known than Micah Clarke," I suggested teasingly. "And the names Arthur Conan Doyle and John Watson will be synonymous with them."

"For the sake of Holmes's career as the scourge of crime, I hope not," Conan Doyle said drily.

He then told us a little more about Wilde's own contribution to *Lippincott's*. It was to concern a man whose

102

physical beauty concealed inner ugliness. A painting of him would hang in an attic to reflect the moral and spiritual decay that never showed on his ever-youthful face. It seemed a most extraordinary idea.

"It is a potent one," Conan Doyle said. "Something elemental, universal lies underneath it. How many of us conceal demons, how much ugliness is there between the superficial beauty of the world. He believes in Aestheticism, rather like that chum of yours in the story, Thaddeus Sholto."

19 September—Dr. Conan Doyle has officially secured the publication of *The Sign of Four* in this *Lippincott's Magazine.* Mr. Stoddart has promised it shall begin its serialization in February of next year. The sum paid to Conan Doyle was considerable, and he has given James half of this.

I was slightly dismayed, though, that James has been omitted from the formal contract arrangements. Neither will he receive credit as co-author of the piece, something with which I took issue.

"There are several reasons for it, Mary. Believe me, it makes for a better arrangement in every respect this way. I came to appreciate its advantages when we collaborated on *A Study in Scarlet.*"

I would not be budged though, and pressed him for a proper explanation. I could tell that I was pushing my luck, but I tried to explain that it was only because I worried about James being taken by this Conan Doyle character.

"Conan Doyle character? What does that mean? The man is a doctor, like myself. The only disreputable doctor I ever knew was Grimesby Roylott, and he was far gone in the extreme."

Turning the subject back to Conan Doyle, I explained, "Well, he's a very charming gentleman, but all that name-dropping and going on about historical fiction. I'm just worried he is depriving you of what you deserve."

"Believe you me, Mary, anonymity is a very favourable situation. I would not care to be like ... well, like Oscar Wilde, for instance, constantly pointed at and gossiped about in every corner. Nor would I wish that upon you. There's also the matter of respectability for a man in the medical profession stooping to write sensational literature, and the danger that might come my way if members of the criminal classes knew of me."

"But won't they know about you when this story is published all across England and America?"

"Honestly, I don't imagine many people will read it. *A Study in Scarlet* didn't get particularly wide exposure, and Arthur doesn't have high hopes—he feels sure historical fiction of the Sir Walter Scott school will be his great literary mark."

"What about what Oscar Wilde said?"

"According to Arthur, Oscar Wilde says that sort of thing to everybody."

29 September—My evening out with James and Arthur will definitely be my last for some time. Of late my energy has dissipated, and the cause is clear. My baby is quite clearly on its way.

Accordingly James has lessened his professional obligations. This was primarily in the interests of assisting Holmes—but benefits me in an ancillary way, as it means he is most often by my side. He has been incredibly solicitous this past little while, and I believe he shall be a very good father.

That is not to say he has been entirely absorbed with my medical requirements. I have totted up the totals, and by my calculation Holmes has been consulted on a good twenty cases this year alone.

On a related subject, James has finally indulged my curiosity and, when he has had a moment and could stay by my bedside, he has read to me some of his accounts. This has provided me with a great deal of stimulation in my growing infirmity.

Even then, though, there are still a few cases that he has forbidden me to look at. Seeing the title 'The Giant Rat of Sumatra' inevitably had me intrigued, but James would not be persuaded about it. "It is a story for which the world is not yet prepared."

"Well, what about 'The Second Stain'? You said I couldn't read that either."

"That one is for political reasons, but the Giant Rat … well, it carries some profound implications that are rather hard to live with."

"You can be so portentous when talking about these things. And yet the title *The Adventures of Sherlock Holmes* gives them an air of excitement. Perhaps after *The Sign of Four* is published, they will want a sequel?"

"It all depends on Arthur, really. You've only to talk to the man to realize that historical fiction will always be his true passion. This is merely something he has a talent for."

"And an obliging friend."

"Some might say that. But perhaps understandably, he thinks he can make more of a name for himself with that than with detective writing. It's much less respected. Aside from Poe and Bret Harte, it tends towards the penny-dreadful end of the literary spectrum."

"Don't be so self-deprecating, my dear. You are a far better writer than any penny-dreadful hack. I'd say you were better even than Poe. And as for Bret Harte—well, I confess I do not know who he is, which makes me even more certain that you are his better."

"Though I do value your opinion, you need only look at those yellow-backed novels and magazines to see the low prestige of the genre. The word 'mystery' is synonymous with cheap hack-work for a sensation-hungry, undiscriminating public."

"But they are not merely mystery stories. 'A Case of Identity', for instance, is a very tragic and romantic story, all about broken hearts and lost love. Whereas 'The Naval Treaty' has the milieu of espionage in it."

"When you are extolling their virtues, I feel like Dickens himself," James said with a blush. "But I doubt they will ever be such a craze."

8 October—At the moment my approaching commitment has made my emotions run higher even than in early January. And while I initially welcomed his presence, I now must have James occupied in some way. The poor man had taken to lingering behind me at all times during the day, which I found rather noisome. Having given him assurance that I will send word as soon as the critical moment arrives, I have instructed him to stay at his club or call on Holmes, until my ill humour passes. It may seem odd to have sent him away when the critical moment draws nearer, but in his present state he is rather like an over-excited horse, quite literally chomping at the bit for his child to arrive.

Later—I am considerably more at ease from a few hours alone. I received this telegram shortly before retiring for the night.

Telegram from Dr. John Watson to Mrs. Mary Watson

> STAYING WITH HOLMES. SMALL MATTER INVOLVING DARTMOOR SUPERSTITION, BASKERVILLES. NO DOUBT TRIVIAL.

10 October—I now feel quite guilty over my respite. James has returned quite gripped with concern over this Baskerville superstition hinted at in his telegram..

"The bald facts of the case are this: Sir Charles Baskerville recently died of a heart attack. There was evidence he was running, and footprints were spied near the body—as he said, 'The footprints of a gigantic hound!'"

"I would agree with your initial impression. An elderly baronet attacked by a wild animal is certainly tragic, but not a mystery of Holmes's calibre."

"Ah, but the hound holds a grim significance for these people. Mortimer told us of the history of the area. The Baskervilles are a very old and dishonourable family. Their manor stands in a benighted part of Dartmoor, near the prison of Princetown. The family's reputation for cruelty extends back to a legend from 1742—when a hound from Hell itself was said to swallow up the profane Sir Hugo Baskerville in the pursuit of an unfortunate neighbour's daughter. Under the circumstances of Sir Charles's death, Mortimer had thought—"

"Had thought that this hell-hound had claimed Sir Charles?"

"Well, Mortimer did not know what to think. I confess that the legend's details are so ghastly, and Mortimer told it with such conviction that I half-believed him last night. In the cold light of day, I remember Holmes's rational outlook and feel rather foolish I paid heed to such arrant mummery.

"This morning, we were visited by Sir Henry. As a Canadian, he sensibly holds little truck with the primitive beliefs stoked in rural England's neglected corners. He received a strange letter, though, telling him to stay away from the moor. Then when we called at the Northumberland Hotel, his boot was stolen."

"So what is your next move? Has Sir Henry heeded the anonymous warning? I take it that no one suspects it could have been written by the dog?"

"He has indeed ignored the warning and is bound for Baskerville Hall."

"And you and Holmes shall go along with him, no doubt?"

"There is a strange matter." James sat and emitted a long and sustained whistle, a tic I knew signalled some long-bottled frustration. "Amid all the oddness of these two days, it is a petty grievance, but there it is. Holmes claims he is too occupied with his cases to travel to Dartmoor at the moment."

"I did not know he was currently occupied?"

"It is the first I have heard of it!"

"So he will leave Sir Henry to fend for himself in his family home? The murderer may well be someone close to him, someone who stands to gain from his death. Such a person could easily have murdered Sir Charles to achieve his aims."

"Ah, but no such person exists. Sir Henry is the sole heir of the Baskerville estate. It is as though that centuries-old curse is succeeding in wiping their ill-starred name from history."

"So, you think Sir Henry is heading to face some spectre?"

"It sounds ridiculous, this hell-hound business, but Mary ... I tell you, what is afoot here is evil, evil in a way that I have seen only once before." He looked away from me. "That is why ... I must accompany Sir Henry to Dartmoor. You would be quite right to hold this against me Mary. I said I would go out of shock more than anything else."

"It sounds as if Holmes will need all the help you can offer him. I do not see a problem with you leaving." The briefest flicker of my sense of adventure from the 'Sign of Four' days resurfaced, and I added, "Of course, I could also accompany you..."

Now it was James's turn to be indignant. "In your present condition? And with this supernatural grisliness all around? No, the farther away you are from any reaches of this business, the better. For your sake, and for mine, it would be better if you stayed here. I have made arrangements with Mrs. Forrester to call on you, and the servants have instructions to cable me if anything happens. I promise you that I shall return to London the second I receive such a message."

I was gripped with concern and pity for my husband. A passing frustration from the previous night has dragged him into all this! Worse, I pushed him away and now Holmes appears to have done the same.

But to think pragmatically, there was no question of me accompanying him. Though Sir Henry would not doubt be a most hospitable host, I was unable to move very far by this point, and long travel would have been far too draining. In addition, James still spoke of the place with a chill in his voice. As keen as he was to write off primitive superstitions, he seemed to be emphatically repeating them like a mantra, as though to stave off his doubts.

As I stood at our front door and wished James success, I saw his current vulnerability laid bare. I held him in my arms for some time. I flatter myself that my intimate farewell had bolstered his spirit somewhat. As James left, he bore his assignment, as he bears all work Holmes heaps upon him, with his usual stoic professionalism.

15 October—How truly bleak! I feel bleak, and the world around me feels bleaker. I have had no word whatsoever from James, and caprice has struck me heavily by causing me to turn for the worse. Physically I can muster no energy, and the London weather has conspired against me by alternating inhospitable levels of rain with lowering skies, so as to prevent even a modest walk down the street.

I at least have taken comfort in the arrangements James made, should my baby make an early appearance. James arranged for Dr. Anstruther to call upon me regularly, and upon his visit the good doctor has assured me that the second any developments occur with the baby, he can be by my side at a moment's notice.

My present condition, however, is not related to the pregnancy. It is a general torpor that visited upon me the morning after James left, and his continued absence has let fester. Were I to know better, I would say this curse was touching myself—why else had I driven James away into its spectral claws? And why else have my spirits so descended?

18 October—So racked with worry am I, both for James and if the baby were to come prematurely, that I have taken to reading James's notes. For the sake of that mystery from January 7, I was disappointed to find the case corresponding to that date—entitled *The Valley of Fear*, with subheadings *The Tragedy of Birlstone* and *The Scowrers*—are empty. Why would James have relocated those notes?

There was also a reference for a book in the collection of the British Museum Reading Room. Its title was *The Dynamics of an Asteroid*, but all the notes written about it suggest it is some highly academic title. James has made a note next to it: "Academic evaluation is that 'No man in the scientific press is capable of criticizing it'". It is probable that it is merely some book that James had marked for leisure reading or as part of Holmes's other researches (since pure mathematics are somewhat outside of James's sphere of interest). I find it hard to believe that there can be anything more than the most abstract connection between this work and a murder in Birlstone.

In the meantime, I concentrated on the case notes that were available. I suppose there is that old wives' tale that reading sensational literature while pregnant is something of a risk. Mrs. Forrester would have me believe that a sudden shock might send the baby out early, and so heaven knows what could have happened from me reading 'The Speckled Band'? I dared not put it down though, as James's narrative skill was so very compelling.

I hope *Lippincott's* publication is a success—these future Sherlock Holmes stories could become a regular feature. There is certainly no shortage of material.

3 November—James returned from Dartmoor late this evening. He was gripped with the frenetic mood that is so typical of him after one of Holmes's mysteries was solved.

"I do think it shall rank among Holmes's most acclaimed cases. Perhaps one day, should *The Sign of Four* succeed, Arthur might let me turn my hand to it?"

"Yes indeed. Tell me every detail about it, James!"

"No," he insisted. "Your term shall end soon, and I shall not risk my own baby by causing a shock to its mother!"

7 November—Once again, Providence struck with its strange precision. In the small hours four nights ago, with James's worry about shocking me still in my mind, I awoke suddenly. I had very suddenly gone into labour, and within minutes James rushed me to St. Bartholomew's

Hospital. He had always been adamant that the doctors there—many of whom were known to him—would be the best equipped to guide me through the birth.

I am sure any woman will say that her own labours must have been the worst ever experienced. Hours without number seemed to pass before finally, this perfect creature emerged. And I am sure any woman will also agree that looking upon the face of one's child made all the agony seem worthwhile.

(Note: There is a large portion missing from the diary here. As Holmes and Watson were not known to be at work on any particularly sensitive cases during these months, it seems likely that it was no more than the vagaries of time. An unfortunate side effect of this, though, is that it leaves blank many details surrounding Mary Watson. It has been difficult to trace any documentation relating to Mary's birth. However, it is reasonable to estimate that she was christened around now, and we are aware that her full Christian name was Mary Victoria Watson. There is the more sinister prospect that some documents were suppressed by Dr. Watson, in view of events to come.)

1890

It may be remembered that after my marriage, and my subsequent start in private practice, the very intimate relations which had existed between Holmes and myself became to some extent modified. He still came to me from time to time when he desired a companion in his investigations, but these occasions grew more and more seldom, until I find that in the year 1890 there were only three cases of which I retain any record.
—'The Final Problem' (1894)

14 January—With Christmas over and young Mary developing very nicely into her second month of life, last week that peculiar mystery again loomed of the events that occurred the day after Holmes's birthday in 1888. Now, though, James was slightly more forthcoming about it.

"It may seem trivial, my dear," James asked me this morning, "but do you recall at our wedding seeing a man you did not recognize?"

"Aside from the groom, you mean?"

"Very amusing, dear. But possibly a thin, academic-looking fellow with a large forehead."

"Now I think you are talking about Holmes ..." At this moment I trailed off, remembering the man who had sent Holmes a card that caused him to depart hurriedly. "Yes, there was such a man. I never got a chance to speak with him. Is it important, James?"

"It seemed so at the time, but perhaps not anymore. Now that two years have passed, I can enlighten you.

Holmes encountered a very evil man, nestled in the heart of respectable society. A scholar, admired by many. And yet beneath his achievements and his quiet, unassuming manner, this man ran a web of crime, vice, and misery that aimed to bring Holmes to his knees, and lay waste to every principle he stood for."

"Is this the subject of that case, *The Valley of Fear*?" I asked.

"Yes. It seemed so trivial, a murder in Birlstone that seemed to be impossible. This criminal managed, though, to orchestrate the entire scheme without even being present. This led to Holmes's desperate pursuit of this arch-enemy, but he seemed to have run aground. I never met him in person, but it gives me quite a chill to think he came so close to my dear wife. Every year when the seventh day of January passes, I think back to those seemingly inconsequential events in Birlstone, and have a shudder at a culprit of such crimes evading Holmes's reach. For if Holmes was not able to catch up with him, mark my words that no human shall."

Unfortunately, as he does in his writings, James left off in mid-stream, as he was called away for a patient. I did not even get the name of this vile master-criminal!

12 February—While real-life assignments to occupy Holmes seem rare at the moment, they have truly exploded as fictional protagonists. For at last, *The Sign of Four* has begun its serialization in *Lippincott's Magazine*. It is strange indeed that this is the first I have read of this crucial tale. In some ways I read it at some remove from reality, as it is filtered through not one but two authorial voices. These many hands explain the occasional errors that mar an otherwise faultlessly written narrative: one particular howler is that the month is described as September at one point, but my character shortly after describes getting the mysterious letter on July 7th! Perhaps it was some attempt to conceal the true nature of the events that happened.

I can only imagine that it was Conan Doyle who added the unflattering description of me and attributed it to Dr. Watson. My dress was described as having "a plainness and simplicity ... which bore with it a suggestion of limited means". Then a few lines down, he mentioned James's "experience of women which extends over many nations and three separate continents".

However, these gripes vanished from my mind as soon as they were followed with: "I have never looked upon a face which gave a clearer promise of a refined and sensitive nature."

Later this week, to celebrate this success—sales have so far outstripped his last publication, *A Study in Scarlet*—James and Dr. Conan Doyle shall attend a dinner with Stoddart. I had to decline, for the sake of attending to little Mary (I have not even left her in the sole charge of the nursemaid yet, which both that good woman and James regard as very strange). Wondering about how much credit Conan Doyle shall get out of all this—as I feared earlier, it is his name alone that appears on the front page—I wondered if Holmes would be attending, as he was the main character in these events.

"No, that would not suit Holmes at all," James insisted. "In fact, he has not spoken to me about its publication at all. He is in truth quite angry about it in many ways. I shall explain the whole story to you later."

I read in the first chapter, Holmes telling of a French detective, Francois le Villard, translating some of Holmes's monographs—'Upon the Distinction between the Ashes of the Various Tobaccos', for example—into French. Before James departed, I teased him that perhaps Holmes was just jealous that James's writing has been more widely read.

17 Feburary—Yet more good news with *The Sign of Four*. Dr. Doyle believes it might be published in book form by the end of the year. I feel I owe the man an apology. In these pages I have been rather sceptical of and hard on him, believing him at first to have taken some attention away from James's accomplishments. The way he venerates historical fiction at the expense of detective stories is a little irksome, and I know James feels demeaned by it. However, in practice he has been unfailingly generous to us both, and seeing the acclaim that James is beginning to receive—deservedly so—I am glad to count him as our friend.

13 April—With *The Sign of Four* gaining more and more readers, I am now receiving letter after letter from old friends and acquaintances. I am in truth vaguely overwhelmed and even embarrassed by the attention. It was obviously necessary for the sake of the narrative that James include the interlude when I discovered the treasure to be lost and he professed his love for me. But reading it, and knowing that this large audience of strangers also will have read it, puts a far different complexion on it.

Coming to realize this, I admitted to James that he was correct not to put his name on the front of the publication. "I can only imagine how inundated Conan Doyle is after all this."

"You and Holmes have slightly more in common than I thought. With this, his name is becoming even more popular. In fact, only the other day, shortly before we were called in to investigate the unpleasant affair of Jephro Rucastle[9], he quite berated me for my prose style. 'You have degraded what should have been a course of lectures into a series of tales.'"

27 April—Idly reading the *Morning Chronicle* over my breakfast, I came across the most curious advertisement. Something called the 'Red-Headed League' is looking for a vacancy, and the members are entitled solely from the colour of their hair, to a salary of four pounds a week for what are called 'purely nominal services'.

---

[9] 'The Copper Beeches', published in the *Strand Magazine*, June 1892.

I considered showing this advertisement to James—to think that he must slave away in his practice when others can be so amply compensated for one's hair colour!

28 June—It does not seem that I have been out of circulation so very long. And yet, this past week having some time to myself with little Mary in the nursemaid's care, it feels as if many years have passed rather than simply a few months. Where do I begin to summarize these momentous changes?

I shall start with the least painful subject. Indeed, it is a matter whose details are downright comic. Holmes and Watson have at last found another stimulating case—although its particulars were particularly eccentric. They were visited by a man with the singular name of Jabez Wilson—who seems a sweet person even though James cannot keep from mocking the simple soul rather harshly (he wrote that he "bore every mark of being an average commonplace British tradesman—obese, pompous, and slow"). Mr. Wilson responded to that advertisement in the *Morning Chronicle* I regarded with such amusement two months ago. It is a timely reminder that everything curious and inexplicable in London will find its way to the 221B Baker Street.

It was as well that they have had such stimulation, as James has grown frustrated with his practice. "It is so un-absorbing these days," he laments. I suspect, therefore, that there was an element of truancy in his traipsing about London with Holmes, visiting Wilson's pawnbroking shop before attending a recital of Pablo de Sarasate at St. James's Hall. All this meandering has proved vital, and tonight James has told me not to wait up for him, as he shall be conducting a vigil at Coburg Square. Any thought that the matter was still trivial firmly evaporated when I saw that he had taken his revolver.

In my own, more mundane circles, I received some very upsetting news from Kate last week. Isa's recovery from opium was short-lived, and he had died just two weeks ago.

"Now that the sad business is done, I can look upon it as a mercy," she said between her tears.

"Did he return to his vice?" I asked.

"Not once. But, after that glorious night when Dr. Watson retrieved him from East London and he returned to me, his eyes full of their former spark, I thought sincerely he could be as he once was. Not that long passed, though, before his condition deteriorated even further. Oh, Mary, if you had seen him in his last days! He was a haunted shadow of his former self, his mind shot to ribbons and his body a hulking ruin. He spoke little, and physically wasted away for months."

"Kate, I feel dreadful. James should have paid him more attention. I remember well feeling very pained at his abandonment of Isa—and, I admit, of us *with* Isa—to pursue some case with Sherlock Holmes."

"Oh, but Dr. Watson did continue to see him for several months. There was nothing he could do, though.

121

The damage had so withered Isa. He was a good friend to me, and to him, as were you, of course."

"I now feel guilty that I have had such a carefree and delightful few months."

Amid her wretched gloom, I was surprised to see this comment elicit a token smile from Kate. "My dear Mary—you always see yourself as such a martyr, as though you should never be allowed any pleasure in life. I cannot think of anyone more deserving of this newfound happiness than yourself, who has contended with her own share of dire hardships. I am particularly pleased you have had a child, as … well, it was another thing denied to Isa and myself."

"Kate, if my marriage to James has taught me anything, it is that it is never too late. Who would have thought that a mere year after my twenty-sixth birthday, content with a few modest positives in my life and all its vast negatives, that I could happen upon a husband, a child, and a whole new life so very soon after?"

One can never know exactly how such encouragement is heard. From the lips of a person blessed with good fortune, they can sound smug and thoughtless. Kate and I, however, have been friends for so long that she knows I meant such sentiments from the bottom of my heart. After our encounter, she came over and met little Mary.

"Of course, the name must have been Dr. Watson's idea," she remarked.

"It was." The words he had said when he explained why—"She reminds me, in her absolute perfection, of the other person I know who bears that name"—struck me as far too sentimental to share with Kate at this moment.

It did send me on a bleak train of thought, though: at the time I was pregnant I thought I was getting too old to bear a child, but now it occurs to me that I am the only woman in my small circle of friends to have one. It makes me appreciate my dear Mary all the more.

17 July—I still talk occasionally with James about Kate's bereavement. Though he was no fan of the man, he has expressed similar sadness. This made the interview we received from Mrs. Hudson all the worse-timed.

I had not seen the Baker Street landlady since October of '88, and she made little attempt to smooth over her earlier, brusque behaviour. In this case, it was for the very simple reason that she was gripped with fear.

"He's dying, Dr. Watson[10]," she wailed as soon as she had sat down in our sitting room. There was no question about whom she was referring. "For three days he has been sinking, and I doubt if he will last the day. He will not let me get a doctor. This morning when I saw his bones sticking out of his face and his great bright eyes looking at me, I could stand no more of it. 'With your leave or without it, Mr. Holmes, I am going for a doctor this very hour,' said

---

[10] 'The Dying Detective', *Strand Magazine*, December 1913.

I. 'Let it be Watson, then,' said he. I wouldn't waste an hour in coming to him, sir, or you may not see him alive."

James told me he had heard nothing of this illness, and it had not even seemed particularly long since he had last seen Holmes without report. At that very instant, he ran to the door and departed for Baker Street with Mrs. Hudson.

I have put Mary to bed, and am trying to get some sleep myself. But if this be the last I hear of Holmes, I shall be so dreadfully sad.

18 July—I anticipated two reactions when James returned home: either he would be inconsolably sad, or filled with delight. It was quite a surprise, therefore, to see him enter with a frown of rage across his features.

"All a trick! Everything he does seems to be some sort of elaborate deception! And I am as much a pawn—no, more a pawn—than any other player! At least his enemies, he treats with respect."

"James, whatever do you mean?"

"I arrived at Baker Street to find Holmes exactly as Mrs. Hudson described him, possibly worse. However, worse even than his physical condition was his temper. He demeaned me as a doctor and demanded that I consult Mr. Culverton Smith. It was his expertise concerning Eastern diseases that made his counsel superior to mine.

"Well, notwithstanding the hurt to my pride and my profession, I did as he asked. Smith appeared to be a courteous and sympathetic man, though I doubt my manner with him was particularly gracious."

"I am not surprised."

"Well, quite. Around he came to Baker Street—and it turned out that he had sent Holmes a very specimen of the Asiatic disease that Holmes was looking for him to cure. Smith meant to murder Holmes!"

I gasped at this turn of events.

"Of course," James grumbled, "Holmes anticipated this all along, and was intending to lure Smith into a full confession of his part in Holmes's attempted murder, and the successful murder of Mr. Victor Savage."

He slumped onto his favourite chair and gave Mary an affectionate tickle. Seeing her always brought some cheer into his eyes. "What a silly thought," he said with surprising bitterness.

"What is that, James?" I asked.

"When we got engaged, I suggested that I should no longer assist him. How silly, therefore, to think that I had any choice in the matter. He will tire of me before I tire of him, and throw me on the heap the moment the whim takes him."

"Now, James, you must not talk like that. Think of how much he depends upon you, think of how much he has given up for you. He would rather you were living with him than with me, and yet he makes the compromise. He would rather numb himself into insensibility with cocaine, and yet for your sake he does not. You must not compare him to a normal person. You must not compare him to yourself." I drew closer and embraced him. "You are far luckier than he is."

"Believe me, I know it."

17 December—The lack of activity my husband and Holmes have been under has now taken on the appearance of the calm before a mighty storm.

With James once again arguing with Holmes (I joked to him how fortunate he is that of his two marriages, ours is the more harmonious; James was not in the mood for such a comment), we have concentrated on little Mary. Her first birthday passed pleasantly, and we are looking into a good school to send her to. I have every reason to believe she will have all the advantages denied in life to me—particularly parents who are close by her. James has made the same vow, and declared that now that he is a family man, it is the right time to lessen his commitment to Holmes.

Of late, he has become somewhat disturbed by Holmes's behaviour anyway. As to my 'calm before the storm' comment, I refer to this master-criminal that they encountered in the *Valley of Fear* case, whom Watson believed had since died. Holmes did not share this belief, and James was fairly certain that this might prove to be Holmes's undoing.

"He first became seized by it at the conclusion of that 'Red-Headed League' business. As you might expect, that foolish Jabez Wilson was being duped. While he was in the offices, being congratulated on his fine head of red hair and distracted in their offices copying out encyclopaedia entries—for which he thought no oddity at receiving four pounds a week!—at his nominal place of business, that pawn-broker's in Saxe-Coburg Square, his assistant was tunnelling underground to gain access to the nearby City and Suburban Bank. Holmes knew that this assistant was in fact John Clay, whom he estimated to be the fourth-smartest man in London with a claim to the third."

"With himself and you as the first and second, no doubt?" I teased. "So, you apprehended this Clay. I remember it. Surely that was an end to the matter?"

"Holmes was dissatisfied with the solution. He has turned the business over in his head again and again. Scotland Yard had to forbid him from going down there and interrogating Clay repeatedly, since his inquiries bore no fruit. Clay was a man of means, you see—he had noble blood. In fact, I marvelled at his blue-blooded effrontery when he berated old Athelney Jones. He said to the poor policeman, 'I beg that that you will not touch me with your filthy hands. You may not be aware that I have royal blood in my veins. Have the goodness, also, when you address me always to say 'sir' and 'please'.' Before being led away in handcuffs, mind you!"

"I am no doubt being slow to see the significance of all this. In what way was Holmes dissatisfied?"

"Ah yes, forgive me. These cases have so many convolutions I sometimes struggle to put them in the right order. The Red-Headed League itself was so meticulously organized, Holmes believed it was beyond the means of even so formidable a mind as Clay's. There were the offices in Fleet Street, the staff of men including Duncan Ross and William Morris, and the ability to procure all the necessary equipment to raid the bank. 'There is the fact that such a talent in the underworld would not go unnoticed and remain freelance forever. And then there is the ... signature upon it. It may not be his work, but it suggests it, as clearly as the brush-strokes of an Old Master.' From there, he has become quite obsessed with what this apparent pattern indicates. And it comes back to his arch-enemy from Birlstone, that mathematics professor.

"You see, Mary, he believes the man's criminal web has only grown. I was inclined to believe him, but he asks too much when he asks Inspector MacDonald to risk his reputation for the sake of these unsubstantiated theories. No one in the C.I.D. will even talk to Holmes about it any more."

"James, you do so easily turn against your good friend. Your best friend, really."

"Do I? How long is my friendship obliged to extend? Months ago, in the aftermath of that 'Dying Detective' case, you mentioned him overcoming his cocaine addiction for my sake. But has this not become a worse addiction? Has the profound reason which lies at the centre of his being not pivoted out of shape, warped itself into these ravings? The streets of London are full of such people. Perched in the speakers' corner of Hyde Park, declaiming every rotten occurrence to be the works of

Anarchists, Baltic revolutionaries, the Jews, the Irish. Any and every scapegoat, offered up to the masses, who convene kangaroo courts to pass judgement. Could there be nothing more than that to this ... this 'Napoleon of Crime' whom Holmes hunts?"

"Did you ever meet him? The Napoleon of Crime, I mean."

"We got close after the Birlstone case. Holmes claims he has been at his heels, and of course there was that fellow at the wedding. But I can see it all too clearly, the man MacDonald describes being an innocent and unsuspecting scholar persecuted by a fanatical detective. Where else would Holmes's mind retreat, faced with so enormous a precept as the world's fundamental lack of reason?

"Remember what he said at the end of the 'Cardboard Box' case, those words that inspired and compelled me to finally proceed with our wedding?"

"How could I forget?"

"The thought that our universe is ruled by chance was, to him, unthinkable. Could he not have been so repelled by the concept that this is where his thoughts have taken him?"

I could hear no more of this. I knew what was happening, and had to stop James before he carried it any further. "You have made an excellent diagnosis ... but of yourself, not of him."

"How dare you, Mary!" he cried. He tried to restrain himself in the presence of our daughter, but I had profoundly shaken him, even more than I intended.

"Please, James, I beg of you to listen to me before you judge. It is indeed possible that Holmes has gone down a rabbit's hole in the pursuit of some reason behind all the purposeless crime that he has made it his business to lend reason to. But are you not, in doubting your best and truest friend, merely questioning your own loyalties? As I have said before, you need not choose between your family and your pre-existing life. Look at our sweet daughter, and remember that she would not be here were it not for the culmination of the unhappy accidents in my life up until July 1888."

James sat silent for some time, and I barely noticed a single tear roll down his cheek. "You are indeed wise, my love," he said simply. "But the decision I have made is final. I cannot be half a man leading two lives. You and Mary are the two most important people in my life now. I am doing you a disservice by my intransigence."

"I know that is not an easy decision to make, and once again implore that you need not make it."

"But you see, Mary ... I know it is the decision I want to make."

1891

"But indeed, if you are trivial, I cannot blame you, for the days of the great cases are past. Man, or at least criminal man, has lost all his enterprise and originality. As to my own little practice, it seems to be degenerating into an agency for recovering lost lead pencils, and giving advice to young ladies from boarding schools."
— *'The Copper Beeches' (1892)*

26 April—In the mail this morning there came a curious correspondence. It was written on high-quality paper, in the delicate handwriting of a refined lady. It did not, however, match the writing or prose style of Kate or Mrs. Forrester, or any other friends. No friend of mine, similarly, would write me an anonymous letter, knowing the unsettling feeling I had when Thaddeus Sholto's missive arrived that fateful day.

> Dear Mrs. Mary Watson,
> I write to you on a matter of some delicacy. I would be very gratified if you would consent to meet with me to discuss matters of importance to you and your family. A single afternoon of your time is, I assure you, all that I require, whatever its outcome may be. I shall be at the Orangerie Teahouse in Kensington Gardens on Thursday at 1:00. I do not mean to disconcert you with this

correspondence and assure you that my intentions are entirely benevolent.

A Friend

James has reconciled with Holmes, although he is still adamant that he will devote more time to his new family when the time is right. Today he was talking with an editor at the *Strand Magazine* named Herbert Greenhough Smith. I am sure this bodes well for future Sherlock Holmes publications, but at the moment it leaves me without anyone to advise me on my course of action. I thus went to see Mrs. Forrester, always a trusted confidante at times like this.

"As you say, it is a woman's writing. So what could the danger be?" she asked rhetorically.

"I am not so sure about that reasoning."

"Well, are there any women whom either you or Dr. Watson may have come into contact with professionally? It may be someone looking for Sherlock Holmes."

"You have something there, Mrs. Forrester. James mentioned someone … Irene Adler was her name, Holmes always knew her as 'The Woman'. Perhaps it could be her?"

Though I still have my doubts, being able to put a face to a name does make me a little more confident about the prospect of meeting this person.

4 May—I am still reeling from this strange encounter. To think that all week I had been avoiding mentioning it to James. My mind was made up after all, and there seemed to be little point in discussing it with him until after it had occurred. Now that it has, though, I scarcely know what to tell him. I came home trembling, and held little Mary tight to my bosom for a long while.

I arrived slightly early in the Strand, and walked into the busy tea room. How strange its mundane operations now seem! Frustratingly, I could see no lady sitting alone, and none present matched the description of Irene Adler. I surveyed the room in an aimless agitation for a few minutes, and was on the point of turning on my heel and leaving.

If only I had!

I had nearly walked back to the entrance, when a man rose from a corner table and walked towards me. His face bore a look of warm recognition, and he beamed at me as he said, "My dear Mrs. Watson, you quite cut me dead. Come, join my wife and myself over here."

"You must be mistaken," I said calmly. I was already uneasy at the sight of the man. His dress, manner, and appearance were the epitome of respectability: a severe black frock coat and stiff collar. He had an ascetic face, and the high forehead hinted—as I am aware from Holmes's interest in phrenology—to a refined intellectual nature.

However, there was something about his manner that made this respectability perverse. Though he gave a consummate performance of recognition and enthusiasm, behind his warm words there was dead-eyed blankness. His upper lip curled into his teeth, in a manner that betrayed some vile appetite—yes, I do not exaggerate when I say that he was trying with considerable effort to suppress thoughts of cruelty and violence that were his nature. The gulf between the performance's authenticity and its sincerity, if that makes sense, held the key to its repulsion.

"No mistake, surely!" he boomed, adding a tenor of bonhomie to his voice. "I arranged it with Doctor Watson himself, though it is a shame he will not be able to join us. Come, come, my dear, please have a seat and the three of us shall have be sufficiently gay in his absence."

He took my arm and led me to his corner table, with just enough pressure to make me feel entrapped. Sitting next to him by the window was a refined lady of about his age. She was plump and attired as respectably as he was. "You of course, remember my wife Gladys," he explained. As with him, I had never seen this lady before in my life, and would certainly have said so had I not locked eyes with this poor woman.

There in her gaze, I saw a coiled spring of desperation and despair. She was trapped here, even more emphatically than I was. She gave her supposed husband a sidelong glance paralysed with fear. Then, remembering her part in this grotesque theatre that had been convened for my benefit, she arched her lips in an over-acted smile and said, "Oh my dear Mary, it is so very good to see you again." The panic beneath her jollity—jollity that had clearly been coaxed from her by force—still fills me with unbridled fear.

As the waiter poured out my tea, and I sipped it uncertainly, the man and his wife made idle and pleasant chat. Then, when the young man departed, the mask slipped away from the man's face.

"Mrs. Watson, I can see you are an unusually intelligent woman. It is no surprise that your husband finds you such … stimulating company." He curled his lip up in an abominable imitation of a smile.

Though I was inwardly quaking in terror, I did my best to retain my composure. "You have the advantage of me, sir. And indeed, I had not expected to meet a gentleman here." I looked sideways at his cowering companion. "There, at least, I remain correct."

My quip—possibly an ill-considered one given my situation—raised his upper lip in gratification again. "Come come, that is a little crude of you to say. I was once a tutor at Dundee University. I am after all a man of means. A man of property." He fixed the woman across from us with a lascivious stare. "To clarify though, this good woman is not my wife, but I felt sure it would set the scene for our encounter the better. And I am something of a stickler for getting these details correct. Unlike that degenerate Holmes, who never once attempts to play the game of respectable society."

Here it was, then. The mention of Holmes triggered an animus in this man I have never seen in a human being. This was beyond hatred, this was a destructive will that reminded me of Lucifer himself when I had first read Milton's *Paradise Lost*. If the comparison seems inappropriate, let me assure you of its gravity while I sat there drinking that infernal tea.

"I take it, then, that you are this Napoleon of Crime?"

"How gratifying, though a touch condescending. Holmes must have given me that honorific."

Not wishing to reveal anything that might compromise Holmes or James, I said nothing. He nodded in a curious gesture of respect.

"James Moriarty, ma'am. Professor James Moriarty, at your service. Do they speak often of me?"

"Hardly at all. If you wish to extract information from me--"

"Come come, my dear Mrs. Watson. What kind of barbarian do you take me for?"

"I only need judge by your handiwork."

For a moment, he did not follow my reference, until he regarded his companion, and then he nodded and emitted a high-pitched bray of laughter. "Oh, my handiwork is considerably more refined than this unfortunate. I am helping her, though, just as I help people of all stripes and walks of life with my actions. Not through the child-like crusade of Holmes, but by a more holistic approach. This good woman, for example, has been blackmailed over a marital indiscretion. A terrible man, Charles Milverton, had acquired indiscreet letters, and I gained their possession in exchange for ... the use of her." He stroked her cheek. She shuddered at the contact, and I could sympathize; Moriarty made the simple pressure of his hand seem like a violation.

"Isn't that obliging of me?" he asked rhetorically. "Her husband shall never know of her wicked ways."

"I beg of you! To carry on in this obscene way!" I exclaimed.

"When our interview is over, she is quite free to go. Just as you are. But that is a fine example. You see, our society depends on people like me to keep its cog-wheels in motion. A cutthroat will only destroy for the contents of a meagre purse, a maniac like Jack the Ripper lashes out to conquer his mental deficiencies. I admire the methods of both but am superior because, you see, I can control. I can bring order to the chaos that was the unruly criminal world of our miserable country. That is what I deplore in Holmes—his coarse and destructive impulses. He would destroy the delicate system that I have created, and bring in its place, what?"

"Sherlock Holmes seeks to restore order, not destroy it. What you describe is nothing more than barbarity."

"Barbarity, you say? Death, poverty, vice, greed. These are barbarities, but ones that exist whether I control them or not. Would it not be better to have a mind such as mine at the top of such a bleak and ugly cycle? As the saying goes, the butcher with the sharpest knife has the warmest heart."

"I cannot accept your reasoning, it is diseased and poisoned by your abnormal world view," I said finally. "Could we come to the point of this interview? You surely need not have dragged me all the way here just to offer a justification for your savage actions."

"That is a fair point. You should thank me, I think, for the generosity I am about to extend to you. You see, I have come here to offer a warning."

"How very common of you. Are you threatening me or my husband?"

"Let us not forget that daughter of yours," he added. My heart missed a beat as he did. "No, no! Once again, you give me such little credit, it is quite hurtful. Mister Holmes and I have waged our war for two years now, and it has reached an intractable *impasse*, I regret to say. Neither my actions nor Holmes's can undo anything at this stage, so I believe I am bound to destroy him."

"You give yourself too much credit—he could and should easily destroy you."

He gave this thought an agreeable nod. "Hmm, your confidence is touching but misplaced. But never mind that. Doctor Watson is a gentleman to whom I bear no ill will. Indeed, in a way I admire his tenacious loyalty—in my own circles I have found few men so thoroughly faithful. I am bound and obliged to destroy Holmes for my own sake, but there is no need to trouble him or you again. A resolution that omitted you from its span you would, I feel sure, find satisfactory. So let me propose this to you. Take your husband away from his sick friend and his morbid obsessions. Let Dr. Watson concentrate on raising his family in peace, and love you as a woman of your calibre deserves. I remember with much affection how happy you looked on your wedding day. I can see the sincerity in both your hearts. Why not put this unhappy business behind you and make him forget all this?"

"Sherlock Holmes is a part of both our lives. I could not ask my husband to betray his friend at this hour of need. And he would never countenance it for a second. I would not expect you to understand such sentiments, it is no surprise to me that loyalty and love are attributes you seldom encounter."

"What a shame. It truly hurts me to hear you say that. These positions are so … untenable. My operations are deeply embedded in the very government of this country. Even a detective of Mr. Holmes's esteem would be unable to destroy such a firm bulwark. Neither he nor Watson have any official backing. My Scotland Yard sources tell me this peccadillo to bring me to justice has greatly jeopardized Holmes's standing with the Force, reduced the poor fellow to a laughing stock. And now they shall both perish. I regret to say that this has also made an enemy of you, my dear. I may in fact need to modify my plans …"

I swallowed, my utter despair and terror taking control of my body. But I would not let this wretched villain see my resolve falter. Whatever happened, I would greet it with dignity. Why had I not told James of my visit here? What if this event gave Moriarty some advantage?

Then, as if to break this hypnotic and sickening nightmare, I heard a clear voice call across the tea room: "Is that Mrs. Watson?"

I turned—only fractionally, lest I let Moriarty out of my line of vision—and saw a red-faced man in drab attire. He walked toward me, removing his shabby bowler hat in deference.

"Tobias Gregson, Mrs. Watson. We met at your wedding, I'm a good friend of your husband and Mr. Holmes."

"Oh yes, of course, Inspector Gregson. Which way are you bound?"

"Funny you should ask, Mrs. Watson, it's your husband's friend Mr. Holmes. Says someone's been dropping bricks on his head in Vere Street, I'm just bound over there."

"What an extraordinary coincidence, I am also!" I beamed at him. I would have flung my arms around him and kissed him, so elated was I. "And of course, Professor, you did promise your good wife that she could accompany me. It would be such a dull afternoon for so distinguished a gentleman anyway, I am sure you are desperate to return to your equations."

The Professor, dedicated as he was to his veneer of respectability, smiled thinly and quietly seethed in his seat as I walked out of the tea room with the poor woman on one side and Gregson on the other. "But Mrs. Watson, I didn't have any tea," he protested.

"I shall buy you all the tea you need," I insisted, "*Somewhere else*, though, I beg of you."

I did not see the other woman again, and can only speculate on her fate. She fled as fast as she could as soon as we reached Gregson's carriage. I began to tell him what had happened, but as soon as the name 'Moriarty' escaped my lips, a fatuous smile of sympathy crossed his lips and he was no longer amenable to anything I would say.

"Begging your pardon, Mrs. Watson, but I really can't let you go on about all this. Holmes and Watson no doubt got to you too," he declared with condescension. "The whole thing will be Mr. Holmes's undoing, I'm afraid. There's no greater admirer than I am of his methods, but it is all quite ludicrous. Still, mind like his couldn't keep pumping away forever, could it?"

After I returned home and held little Mary in my arms—oh, what an utter relief it was to see her—I rushed into James's examining room. I was no doubt in a somewhat dishevelled state, and so he escorted me into his other room and left his baffled-looking patient.

I told him the whole horrifying incident, not holding back my sobbing. He nodded gravely.

"Once again, Mary, to think that I doubted him and you retained your faith. Which of us is the more loyal friend?"

"There is no question, James, that you must help him purge this ... cancerous individual from his place in London's criminal underworld."

"I am so glad to hear you say that," cried the patient from the other room. Scarcely noticing him, I was as startled as James was to see him slip putty from his face

141

and reveal himself as Sherlock Holmes. "Your daughter Mary saw through it at once, I must admit. She was winking at me frantically as I crossed the stairs."

After he drew the blinds, Holmes proceeded to explain that Moriarty had been to see him the other day. He reported their encounter with a matter-of-fact terseness that belied its colossal import. "Now then, Watson, since your last patient has made, shall we say, something of a recovery, I must move at once."

"You will spend the night here?" James asked.

"No my friend, you might find me a dangerous guest. I have my plans laid, and all will be well." There was a definite tremble of doubt in his voice, but he continued to outline his plans with his usual precision. The only other sign of fragility was his deference to me at the end of his programme, when he asked, "There is only the small matter, then, of your wife's permission?"

"Of course you have it." I put a hand on each of their cheeks, a gesture I felt Holmes shrink in discomfort at. "Do whatever is necessary, gentlemen. I wish you Godspeed."

Later—With Holmes in pursuit of Moriarty, James can tell me nothing of his movements. "Even I do not know anything of them. He wouldn't even leave through the front door, instead he hopped over the garden wall."

"Will he be safe?"

"His brother's rooms at the Diogenes Club are, by his estimation, the safest and most inviolable walls in all

142

England. And he needs not worry about its members speaking out of turn about any unusual guests[11]. Tomorrow I am bound for the Lowther Arcade."

With Holmes gone, and with such fear in both our hearts, we passed the night once more in marital intimacy. For these all too brief moments, it seemed as though all would be right in the world. But then, an hour later, James rose and dressed. His long journey—Holmes's final problem—was set to begin.

Many months ago I had begun a tapestry. It is in truth an ugly thing, and I had put it away unfinished. But today, it felt right to take it out and complete it. There is something in this quest of theirs that brings to mind the *Odyssey*, and as much to spare myself from the thought of the death that these dear men dance with, I am instead trying to think of myself as a virtuous Penelope, at her knitting, her life consumed with hope for the day when her love returns.

I sit and wait ...

(As far as can be determined, Mary recorded no further diary entries this year. Her next entry picks up recapping from this point. But from an historical perspective, July 1891 may be the most important date in Sherlockian history to this point. For it was then that the

---

[11] The Diogenes Club, as Holmes explained in 'The Greek Interpreter' (1893), was founded for "the most unsociable and unclubbable men in town. No member is permitted to take the least notice of any other one. Save in the Strangers' Room, no talking is, under any circumstances, allowed."

Strand Magazine *published 'A Scandal in Bohemia', the first of its series entitled* The Adventures of Sherlock Holmes. *For it was here that the detective's fame, and indeed his immortality, was cemented.*)

1892

It is with a heavy heart that I take up my pen to write these the last words in which I shall ever record the singular gifts by which my friend Mr. Sherlock Holmes was distinguished ... It was my intention ... to have said nothing of that event which has created a void in my life which the lapse of two years has done little to fill.
— *'The Final Problem' (1894)*

19 April—Can there be an opening line in all literature that has such hidden complexity, and such truth to life, as Dickens' immortal: "It was the best of times, it was the worst of times"?

This is the first time I have dared to take up my pen since those momentous, dreadful events of nearly a year ago. Only now do I feel sufficiently fortified to sift through its wreckage and extract both the good and the bad from it.

There is, regrettably, only one place to begin—that fateful day last May when James returned from Switzerland, alone. Moriarty had lured him away to Meiringen with word of a sick patient, and he and Holmes both plunged to their deaths in the Reichenbach Falls. When James returned, he said nothing about it for days, and indeed was very relaxed and light-hearted. He was quite his old self as he asked myself and little Mary about her week (she is talking quite a lot these days).

145

Soon after, there was all the business of Holmes's funeral, which was sombre and poorly attended. His brother Mycroft, Mrs. Hudson, and a handful of ne'er-do-wells from around London, who were touchingly gratified by the benefit Holmes had given to their lives and situations, paid their respects.

Mycroft was an even more distant and alienating figure than his brother, and hovered on the fringes but talked to no one aside from James. James—who was welcomed at the event almost as a brother—remained cordial but taciturn throughout, and became even more so when the will was read and his modest bequest was acknowledged.

Oddly, Mycroft has continued to rent the rooms in Baker Street from Mrs. Hudson. Perhaps they shall stand as a monument to his feats in detection, much as Dr. Samuel Johnson's house in Gough Square has become a shrine to logomaniacs and lexicographers from far and wide.

A few days after all this, with the dust settled, I saw fit to ask him about Holmes.

"Yes, yes," he said lightly. I was somewhat taken aback by his casualness, but then he added: "Don't you see, Mary, it is all that Holmes wanted. As he said himself in his … his last note to me, that it was the most fitting way he could see of concluding his life's work. In a way, I cannot begrudge him that wish … so painful though it was to me."

I thought back to that horrible day before they left. It made me glad—in a grim way that I did not enjoy feeling—that the man who had perpetrated all that misery was now finally perished, and that no more lives would be ruined by the poisonous shadow of Moriarty. And part of what made Holmes so very special was that he considered it worth the cost of his own life to eliminate that evil for all time.

I wonder, however, how long this façade shall hold up. James is clearly wracked with emotional torment about all this. I had fully prepared to nurse him through this difficult recovery. I know that he is bottling up his true feelings with that famous stoical reserve that he has shown so many times. Usually, though, he has permitted me to see him with that guard down, but not in this case. I wonder, and worry, about why this could be.

It cannot be helping James's grief that, in another way, Holmes is very much alive. Shortly before he departed to Switzerland for Holmes's 'Final Problem', James consulted with Herbert Greenhough Smith, editor of the *Strand Magazine*. Further to that meeting, since last July, James's reminiscences have been running in that periodical, with Arthur Conan Doyle once again acting as editor, literary agent, and *de facto* co-author. So far nine *Adventures of Sherlock Holmes*, as they will be called when published in book form this October, have been published—from 'A Scandal in Bohemia' to 'The Engineer's Thumb', taking in 'The Red-Headed League', 'The Blue Carbuncle', and 'The Man With the Twisted Lip' amongst others.

I thought the popularity of *The Sign of Four* was quite inconceivable, but this! Herbert has been around

147

several times to congratulate James on his excellent work. Though the exact figures have yet to be calculated, he is willing to estimate that Sherlock Holmes—or rather, as he indelicately put it, Conan Doyle's name on the magazine's cover—has added 100,000 copies to its circulation!

I can well believe it. Whenever I am about town with either James or Arthur, they are stopped in the street by admirers. Though Arthur has scathingly said, "I don't know how they recognize Dr. Watson here. Those illustrations are awful! I had wanted Walter Paget but ended up with his brother Sidney."

"I must say, Mr. Paget gives Sherlock Holmes a very handsome likeness," I opined.

"Aye, that's where he goes wrong," Arthur objected. "Still, all those women readers of the *Strand* seem—ridiculous though it is to say it—quite taken with that caricature they see every month."

"And what about my likeness?" James asked. "Do I look more handsome on the page than in person?"

"Well, that would be quite impossible," I dutifully riposted as I kissed him on the cheek. I dare say Arthur groaned at this.

The good news does not stop there. Arthur has made additional money from the American publication (as well as a New York edition of the *Strand*, they have been syndicated in several American papers). We passed Baker Street one morning, and saw line-ups of people outside, staring up at those empty rooms of 221B.

"They have a word for these people in America," Conan Doyle muttered darkly. "They call them 'fans'."

"Why ever would they name them for those folding devices to cool one's skin?" I asked.

"It is a shortening of the word 'fanatic'."

25 May—An odd conversation with James today. He has become ever more distracted, and gives little attention to little Mary, myself, or even his patients. He has generally neglected me as a wife also, and I have taken to elaborately hinting that another child may settle this imbalance.

We have never had any difficulty in communication before. And I know exactly why it is—but every time I bring up the subject of Holmes, James merely clamps shut and will talk of other matters like a man possessed.

That made our discussion today all the more remarkable. Sadly, it was far from an amiable subject. "Do you know," he began, "I feel quite better about Holmes. I know you have worried about me a bit these last few months my dear, but I am sure that I have solved it."

"I have indeed worried about you, but I know how hard it must be to put all those terrible events behind you."

"That is what I thought as well. But today I realized that I do not have to."

"Why is that?" I asked, trying to keep the concern from my voice.

"Well, it occurs to me. I did not see Holmes go over the side of the Reichenbach Falls. I was called away and

149

returned to find this note. What if Holmes had gotten rid of Moriarty, survived, but wanted the world to think he was dead? For the purposes of sorting out Moriarty's gang and so forth."

"So you doubt whether Holmes is dead?"

"Emphatically. In fact, I believe he is probably at large in London. I'm sure he is disguised somewhere and will come out of the woodwork when the time is right. But it makes it quite impossible, my dear, to consider having any more children with you."

My heart quite sank when I heard these words. "Why is that?" I asked as blandly as possible.

"Well, little Mary—though I am charmed and blessed by her presence every minute of her life—is already quite a commitment on my part as a father, and indeed upon you as a mother. I must be ready, furthermore, at any time to pick up Holmes's gauntlet and resume our adventures. You yourself said that we should never leave each other's side, and I hope you are as good as your word!"

I have been to see Arthur about this, and though it is somewhat outside his expertise, he has given me some draughts to help James sleep. Some nights I hear him prowling and pacing downstairs, and once, I was certain I heard muffled sobbing.

13 June—Little Mary continues her progress, and will begin this autumn in school. She has become a polite and charming young lady, and wherever possible I have been there to look after her. I remember my own isolated upbringing all too well.

"You are very good to me Mummy," she said with that delightful candour that children are so expert at.

"And what about your father? Is he good as well?"

"Oh yes. But we cannot expect too much of him, Mummy."

"Why is that?"

"He does miss Mister Shylock so very much." Understandably for a toddler, she finds Sherlock Holmes's name difficult to say. "I don't think he'll be better until Mr. Shylock comes back."

"Do you think he will come back?"

"Daddy thinks he will. And Daddy must be right about that, because he is one of the cleverest people I know. We are all very lucky, we Watsons. Probably you and I got it from Daddy being such good friends with Mr. Shylock."

24 June—With the last of the twelve *Adventures of Sherlock Holmes* published, James had another of these brainstorms. He has lately been obsessing over the publication schedule, and Arthur and Herbert have been so very accommodating to get him so involved. In truth, there is little he can contribute to these meetings, but both men know it is helping James along.

I feel far better today than I have for some time. James and I had a long conversation about the state of affairs for the last little while.

151

"I realized what a damn fool I have been acting," he began. "I was out on a call by Aldersgate Street, and I saw past the usual peddlers and vendors this old bookseller. I was positive that it was Holmes. I walked past him a couple of times, and then I whispered in his ear. He talked back to me, and I congratulated him on his uncanny performance. One of his best disguises yet. I waffled on and on, and this bookseller started looking at me as though I was mad. It was like … it was like that time we went to Brighton …"

The walls then finally broke down, and the tears he had been holding back so very long gushed forth like a tidal wave.

"How desperately, *desperately* I wanted not to believe it, or to believe that it would not affect me!" he cried. "Oh, everything is so dreary, so totally and entirely *dreary* now. What do I do? Mary, for the love of God, what do I do?"

I felt so wretched consoling him, for even then I was left with a twinge of wounded pride. I decided to treat him with equal candour, and say what I felt. "I feel responsible," I admitted. "I feel I have let you down as a wife, letting you decline to this terrible state."

He wiped the tears from his eyes and seized me in his arms. "Mary, how can you possibly say that? You are the best and wisest woman I have ever known, but you still get things abominably wrong sometimes!" He laughed at this, the first and most genuine laugh he has had in a long while.

"Tell me why," I replied, smiling at his improved spirits.

"I owe the shreds of sanity and self-worth that I still have to you, my truest love. I think of Holmes and all I can think is how I let him down, how my absence contributed to his death—no matter how much he intended it to be so, I should have known, I should have been sharper! But seeing you and Mary, and the joy and love that I continue to get from you daily ... the world has for so long seemed such a grey and lacklustre place. That veil of evil that seemed to descend on the metropolis last January has lifted, but it is as though gauze still remains in place, making everything fuzzy and blurry, vague and distorted. Just a miasma of banality. Into that miasma, though, comes down these shafts of brilliant bright light. They remind me what it was all for. *You* remind me what it was all for. Now let me take you at once to bed, and I shall set about obliging your most recent nuptial request."

Entering into the spirit of this humour he was now in, I admitted, "You have neglected your obligations in that matter for rather a long while."

28 June—To echo James's metaphor, it feels as though that veil has fully lifted! We went to Brighton, and never have those beaches and piers seemed so gloriously sunny in all my visits there!

When James had gone to fetch us some ice cream, little Mary decided to broach the subject of her father's improved humour.

"He has come to terms with some difficult facts," I said, trying to be as vague as I possibly could. I did not, after all, want to upset my daughter having just healed my husband.

"It's Mister Shylock, isn't it?" little Mary asked. "He's not coming back after all."

"No he is not," I said simply. I looked at her as I would look upon a friend, desperate for some sympathy or words of wisdom. The clever little creature that she is, she recognized this entreaty at once.

"Then we shall have to look after Daddy even more than before," she concluded. "He only has us to depend on now."

I held her close to me, and laughed and cried. "Yes, I could not have said it better myself, Mary. That is exactly what we must do."

"I think I'll be better at it than you," she then remarked.

15 December—We are flush with good news at the moment, with the book edition of *The Adventures of Sherlock Holmes* continuing to sell well and the *Strand* publishing another twelve with the title of *The Memoirs of Sherlock Holmes*. To think that, a few months ago, he was toying—quite indelicately, I must say—with the idea of adding Holmes's death to the end of 'The Copper Beeches'. His mother had dissuaded him from this. But now, more Holmes stories shall come—and what is the more remarkable in fact, Greenhough Smith was so desperate for

154

Arthur to do another series that he has paid him £1,000! If ever there was proof of the craze for Sherlock Holmes, this is it! I cannot imagine the demand and the downright hysteria for these detective stories continuing past that, but who knows?

With our share of this bounty, James has surprised me with a treat. Over Christmas, we shall go away to Switzerland with the Conan Doyles. Arthur has been telling him all about skiing and James is awfully keen to have a try at it.

26 December—James is somewhat slower to adapt to skiing than Arthur, but I keep telling him that his war wound gives Arthur the advantage. The Conan Doyles' daughter Mary Louise, is the same age as our little Mary, so the two have become great friends. Arthur's wife Louise— 'Tooie', as he calls her—has been quite unwell. She attributes this to the strain placed upon her by travel, and so recently giving birth to their second child Kingsley. As a result, though, I have spent most days with her, and I think she has welcomed some company.

One evening, when James and I were walking about in this magical Swiss village, the true spirit of Christmas all around us, he said to me, "Mary, I am truly sorry I have neglected you as a husband. I know you will deny it fervently but I mean to turn over a new leaf."

"You do not know I would deny it. Perhaps in parts I agree, but I understand why."

"You always have my dear. And I hope that our family can enter this new year with its demons behind it."

31 December—Emotions have run higher than might be expected for holidaying Britons. On Hogmanay, Arthur and James imbibed rather heavily, and became very verbose (as I know from experience James is apt to do, although it seldom happens).

"My dear Louise, my dear Mary, do either of you know exactly what it was that brought old Watson here and myself together? What made friends of us?"

We both confessed that we did not. James made an aggravated cough, that I knew to be his inarticulate attempt to abort this topic of conversation. Arthur merely raised his voice to talk over the noise.

"Louise, I have of course told you of my dear father. Mary, you are no doubt familiar with John's brother Henry."

"Yes indeed."

"Now Arthur, there's no need to go into all of that," James protested.

"Old Watson—old *John* here—well, that was it. In this world, when you have a weakness like the drink, it doesn't matter what else you do. My father was a talented artist you know. I tried so hard to help him however I could."

James turned to me. "He got him to illustrate *A Study in Scarlet* you know. I never quite forgave him for giving Holmes that giant beard."

156

As we all laughed, Arthur added, "Father has a giant beard you know. Didn't believe Sherlock Holmes was real, he thought I'd based the character on him!" Then he became serious once again. "But John here, he knew. It was the same with Henry."

"Yes indeed. And you were a great help to me during the worst of those years. I hope I was the same to you."

"Of course you were, man! That's what has made you such a good doctor."

"You are both good doctors," I added.

"I don't know how good a doctor I am," Arthur remarked with a blush. "All that fame that Sherlock Holmes, and the good Doctor Watson here, have gathered is in some part due to my lack of success."

"Oh, don't say that Arthur!" Louise remonstrated.

"No, no, Tooie, it's true. I came to London last year, determined that tuberculosis would be my area of speciality. I went to Viennese lectures, took as many notes as I could with my limited understanding of German. But I was convinced—convinced, I tell you—that this was where my future lay. So I packed up my practice in Southsea and started one up in Devonshire Place. Not a single patient came, not one! So I turned back to Herbert at the *Strand* with those two stories Watson had given me."

"Well then, your professional loss is the gain of the world of literature," I said.

"Damn it all though, I wouldn't have done it without Watson here," Arthur continued. James was now even more embarrassed at his friend's over-affection, but I always find him somewhat adorable in this state so saw no problem in his friend continuing. "I never saw the potential of the Holmes stories, still can't quite fathom how immensely successful they are. I owe that to you John."

"You've considerably helped me too, Arthur."

"Aye. Without good friends, I tell you," Arthur said, "All you've got are your weaknesses and then, there you go. My father's still around, but he doesn't have long[12]. And your brother went the same way. No one can understand if they haven't seen it themselves."

Louise put a sympathetic hand on Arthur's shoulder, but he pulled himself up stoically and raised a glass. "It is Hogmanay, so perhaps it would be appropriate. How about a toast as we bid farewell to the year to all those absent friends?"

So we did, to Henry Watson, to Isadore Whitney, and lastly to Sherlock Holmes.

---

[12] Charles Altamont Doyle did indeed pass away in 1893.

1893

"Your fatal habit of looking at everything from the point of view of a story instead of as a scientific exercise has ruined what might have been an instructive and even classical series of demonstrations. Your slur over work of the utmost finesse and delicacy, in order to dwell on details which may excite, but cannot possibly instruct, the reader."
— *'The Abbey Grange' (1904)*

12 January—It has been a slow start to this New Year. Truly I have felt very frail ever since I returned from Switzerland. At first I believed it was simply because that time had been so joyous and physically invigorating, but as the weeks have passed I am beginning to worry about other things. This may be my new permanent condition, or it may even pave the way for still worse declines. At the moment there is no particular reason to worry though. I have not troubled James with it, as he has been hit rather hard with returning to a full workload and more *Strand* obligations.

Arthur has helped him considerably with the polishing of his manuscripts for what are now being called *The Memoirs of Sherlock Holmes*. He has been over most nights, and James will frequently finish a long day's work as a physician before rolling up his sleeves and toiling away on getting a Holmes case into narrative order.

It is quite a captivating spectacle to watch the two men at work together. James has ample concentration, but needs Arthur's polish to put the accounts into a pleasing form. While Arthur has the more inventive prose style, he is the more easily distracted. Therefore, their collaboration is very congenial to both.

Today, for instance, he asked whether we had read in the paper of some of the exploits of a Norwegian by the name of Sigerson. "A very prodigious traveller—he has passed through Persia, Mecca, even as far as Khartoum. Now there is a fascinating character. I sometimes think when we finish these Sherlock Holmes accounts, I shall pen a tale of explorers, discovering some unknown corner of the globe. Somewhere even more exotic than Khartoum."

"Yes, well, let's get these finished before you start thinking about what you'll be doing next!" was James's exasperated reply.

I feel it is a great pity, but both men are adamant that this new series of twelve should be the end of the Holmes publications. James has selected the best examples of his friend's gifts—including two, that I am quite thrilled to read, from Holmes's University days—and believes that 'The Naval Treaty', with its international intrigue, and particular deductive feats on the part of Holmes, is the perfect finale for the series.

"Is there any chance that you shall write of 'The Final Problem'?" Arthur asked, with considerably more tact than the question appears written down.

Something of the emotion that had so tortured James resurfaced. "I know you may think my reasons for not wishing it published are entirely personal."

"My dear," I interjected, "surely you may publish whichever stories you want."

"I concur, and please don't think I meant to stir up those old ghosts for you," Arthur quickly added.

"It is not that, although a part of me does think it is right to spare the reading public the … the unvarnished grief that the incident stirs with me. Part of me feels that it would be … rather nice for everyone to think that Holmes is still alive and well. But no, I do not think of those reasons. I merely think the concept of Professor Moriarty, and his sinister web of crime, is best left unrecorded."

"Why?" Arthur asked. "Moriarty is dead too remember, all the remaining members of his gang were caught by the police."

"That we know of," James cautioned. "But no—to learn of such all-encompassing ill descending on London. It is one thing to report on crimes of an individual nature, but it is quite another and, I think, a more unsettling matter to have the bulwark of society and civilization revealed to have such a serpent lurking in its midst. Indeed, even controlling it. Moriarty is an unsettling idea, and I would rather he remain unrevealed."

Arthur agreed at James's assessment and the two men quickly began talking of 'The Naval Treaty', and organizing Holmes's two first-person accounts—those University anecdotes, entitled 'The "Gloria Scott"' and

161

'The Musgrave Ritual'—into a more thrilling, less academic style.

"That was Holmes to the end," James chuckled. "No doubt even from beyond the grave he will be withering at my attempts to turn 'what should have been a course of lectures into a series of tales'."

31 January—Very sad news indeed today. Louise's illness has not abated, and it seems likely she has contracted tuberculosis. Arthur has been inconsolable, and has withdrawn from further work on the Holmes stories to care for his wife. I believe this dreadful news has affected him even more personally. He berates himself in the harshest possible turns, going on that he should have seen the signs when she gave birth to Kingsley, and his medical skill has again let him down. I think he is being still harder on himself because it was the very disease he had wanted to specialize in.

In any event, and with most of the remaining *Memoirs of Sherlock Holmes* prepared for publication, Arthur has retreated to Switzerland again. It has strengthened his resolve that he has neither the time nor the inclination to publish further Sherlock Holmes cases. Mr. Greenhough Smith, ever chipper, said to him as we bade them farewell: "For the sake of Holmes, for the sake of my readers, Arthur, you must get your wife well again! That's an order, damn you!"

My own condition grows worse, and though it seems selfish to dwell on it in the wake of a dear friend facing something so intractably hopeless. Little Mary was most distressed, as she has become very close with the Conan Doyles' daughter Mary Louise, and the child has been dreadfully sad about the whole business.

"You'll soon get better, won't you Mummy?" she asked me.

"You can depend on it," I assured her. Though lately I have been dubious—every day does seem to deteriorate on the day before it.

17 February—For the first time in many months, I travelled to Camberwell to visit Mrs. Forrester. Though she has a slight cramp that has given her a stick, she is still the same healthy and energetic woman I knew and loved so well.

"You have let me down awfully, Mary," she mockingly scolded me. "When can I expect you to resume your post as governess? The ladies I've had to replace you are fairly hopeless. And the students don't seem to respond as well to them as to your fair features."

"I hope I was more than just a pretty face to my pupils," I rebutted.

"Ah, Mary, there is no disguising your serious moods. You do get so very serious." Mrs. Forrester seemed to see something in me, something I was not aware of myself.

I explained to her about Louise Doyle, and how I seemed to be so very enervated of late. "Therefore, Mrs

Forrester … knowing you and valuing your friendship so highly…"

"Please Mary, the friendship is equally valued on my part. Anything I can do to be of service, you need only name it."

"Well, I anticipate … in the worst-case scenario, I may leave my daughter, my dear little Mary, without a mother. It is about her that I worry. And though I am sure James would be perfectly capable and willing a parent, there are some aspects of his life that are not congenial to the rearing of a child."

"Say no more—I've always thought he could never be as full a husband or father as you and Mary deserved with Sherlock Holmes sharing his affections."

In line with James's wishes, I had not even told my dearest friends of Holmes's current whereabouts. As well as his personal problems coming to terms with this, he also rationalized that if it was known Holmes was dead, the criminal community would rejoice, and it may even lead to a resurgence of Moriarty's organization (one or two members, he was sure, had evaded justice). It was another reason he did not wish to publish 'The Final Problem'—he wished Holmes to remain an immortal symbolic bulwark against evil in all its forms.

Sitting in Mrs. Forrester's Camberwell sitting room, though, this explanation was very inconvenient. Therefore I had to sit in silence and suppress my sorrow to hear his name so besmirched by my good friend.

"That aside, Mrs. Forrester—though with your objections noted—I wonder if I could rely upon you to take little Mary into your care."

"It would be utmost honour, Mary. In fact, I have always considered myself a mother to you."

"I have thought of you that way also," I hastily added.

"So it would be second nature to take another Morstan into my care, and if I had any hand in making you half the lady you are today—so very kind and generous, and loving to Dr. Watson, which I hope he appreciates—I should be happy to make the same contribution to the next generation."

"I am deeply in your debt, Mrs. Forrester."

"Not at all!" she exclaimed, her sincerity once more coated in her trademarked bluster. "We are talking about an extremely hypothetical situation. And I for one think it will be more likely that you will be banging on my door in a couple of months looking for work. And as I've said before, with the sorry lot I have now I'll be forced to take you on no matter what extortionate terms you ask!"

With perfect timing, at this point one of Mrs. Forrester's hapless governesses entered the room with her face covered in India ink. "I can't handle them monsters!" she declared in thinly concealed Cockney.

21 March—James has been much distressed by an item today in the *Pall Mall Gazette*. Sadly, if inevitably, the incredible fame of Sherlock Holmes has attracted some unsavoury attention.

Colonel Moriarty Attacks Sherlock Holmes, Defends Brother's Legacy

It seems these days vulgar celebrity is allowed to excuse all manner of unsavoury personal behaviour. Month after month, the readers of the *Strand Magazine* thrill to the exploits of the detective Sherlock Holmes. The Prince of Wales himself is rumoured to be among their number. So skilful is the writing and presentations of his actions that they have become misunderstood, to the extent that many of his readers believe him to be a fictional character.

If only he were, I think to myself with a heavy heart!

Even on his own, this detective cuts rather a sinister figure. He has all of the trappings of a gentleman but none of the proprieties. He scorns respectability; he makes a mockery of the conduct and deportment our society is founded upon; he treats our most sacred institutions with suspicion; he will consort with lowly ruffians in the pursuit of his dubious aims. Were I not informed of his friend and colleague Dr. John Watson's marriage, I would also regard his erstwhile living arrangements with this gentleman highly questionable as well.

However, all of these characteristics—though no doubt objectionable to citizens of any common decency—are no more than his personal choices. I do not wish to censure Mr. Holmes for this. I was, however, grieved that a private correspondence I had written to a friend found its way into a newspaper, and was given a suitably gaudy headline. My letter merely expressed similar opinions to those I have written above, and I feel as a citizen in a free country, I need not apologize for having expressed them. However, the opprobrium that greeted my words was such that I have become a pariah.

The purpose of this open letter, therefore, is to make public allegations against Mr. Holmes that simply cannot stand unchecked. The good name of my family—that of Moriarty—has been stained by its involvement and persecution from this incorrigible rogue. Worse, I have lost a brother.

The facts are these. In the later months of last year, Mr. Holmes used his unjustly lauded reasoning skills to make the grotesque and wholly unfounded allegation that my brother, a respected former Chair of Mathematics at Dundee University, orchestrated and enacted criminal enterprises. The scope of these schemes was international and the motivation unclear.

Using the leverage his previous victories have afforded him with Scotland Yard officials, Holmes was able to launch a probe, without any foundation, into Professor Moriarty's activities. By their own admission, the C.I.D. found no evidence whatsoever of even circumstantial evidence to match the gravity of these charges. One Inspector MacDonald made repeated inquiries about Professor Moriarty.

Had the matter ended there, it would have been an embarrassment and an inconvenience only. Even the mild harassment would, in this context, be tolerable. But Holmes would not accept his failure, and refused to let the matter rest. The severity and intensity of his persecution continued, until Professor Moriarty saw no alternative but to convene an interview with Holmes. This he did quite literally fearing for his life—a fear that our family now knows was all too justified.

Mr. Holmes plainly stated to the Professor that he saw no alternative conclusion to their status quo but to act as an executioner, in order to rid the world of the invidious presence of such a master criminal. Again, it chills my bones—as a retired soldier and an Englishman—that there are in our civilization men who feel justified in perverting the law solely to satisfy an insane blood lust. Worse, that the law would actively allow such a deranged individual to pursue this course of action.

Not surprisingly, I think, Moriarty fled England altogether, telling no one of his movements (not even myself). It may seem an extreme reaction but it attests, I think, to the raw and unvarnished terror that the Professor now held.

But, as readers of his chronicles in the *Strand* are all too aware, Holmes is no ordinary mortal. He was able to piece together the Professor's secret flight and continue his pursuit. That he could apply his admittedly impressive skills to such an aim is nothing short of perverse, and speaks to me of the depth of his aberrant mental condition.

It was at the Reichenbach Falls in Switzerland that Holmes finally caught up with Professor Moriarty. There, his harassments continued to physical violence, which ended with both men tumbling into the Falls to their deaths. The matter of Holmes's death has for some reason been little reported. A brief précis in the *Journal de Geneve* and a Reuter's dispatch are the only accounts I am able to find, and shamefully both seem to imply that this was some unforeseeable accident, rather than the outcome of systematic persecution from a dangerous and mentally unbalanced individual.

Seeing as these reports were little circulated (apparently Holmes's brother is a government official, another testament to the insidious infiltration of the Holmes family into our respected seats of power), I finally would like to set the record straight. My brother was a dedicated and brilliant scholar. Military and academic colleagues have sent their sympathies from far and wide at his passing. Colonel Sebastian Moran, a business associate and family friend, spoke fondly of the Professor's meticulous nature, his taste in art, and also the high standard he brought to all his work. "The Professor often said that the mark of a true master was invisibility. He did not wish to be in limelight, but off to the side, to effect change from the background."

A fellow scholar, John Clay—a peer of the realm who was sent to jail by Holmes's chicanery—said, "Professor Moriarty had great ambitions. It is a great sorrow to me that he never had the opportunity to leave his mark on the world as he ought to have. Mark my words, the scope of his vision would have created a great change that would have reverberated across all England."

I appreciate such words, but as you may imagine, they are a small consolation as I continue to live with the turmoil of a dear brother, taken from me so very senselessly. I hope all readers, and all Englishmen, can understand how very obscene it is that his murderer is so valorized.

Sincerely,
Colonel James Moriarty

I had to say that when he threw the paper on the table in front of me, I frankly told James that it was of little merit, and he should not worry over it. "The whole thing is so patently false. Even the most casual reader of Sherlock Holmes's stories would recognize the falsehood of Colonel Moriarty's claims. It is quite simply your word against his, and few would have any reason to take him at his word. And even this Colonel's character makes me suspicious. Did not Professor Moriarty have the Christian name of James?"

"Oh, Mary! I wish I could believe you!" he cried. I have truly never seen James fume with anger, pain, and sorrow quite so raw as after he read this letter.

I tried my best to reassure him. "Please, James, no one will pay him any heed. After all, everyone in England—and America, even—knows and loves Sherlock Holmes. And you and I know the true events."

"It is so terribly unjust, Mary. The indignity of it— attacking my dear friend, who cannot even defend himself! To think that he died, and respect cannot even be paid to what he died in the aid of!"

"We both know of the depth of Professor Moriarty's actions," I said, careful at the sentiment I was expressing. "However … is it not in some ways reasonable that the man's own kin would take an unfavourable view of Holmes? No one with a keen awareness of Moriarty's criminal activities would risk defending his actions so publicly."

"But what he said about Holmes! Had he restricted himself to his brother's reputation, I would have seen it for the lie it was, but I might have understood it as you say— even if I would still have found it morally repugnant. And without full possession of the facts, it would be very easy to turn the tide of public opinion against him. To think! While Moriarty was weaving his trail of mayhem and destruction—even the dreadful attentions he paid you that day before we went off to chase him to Switzerland! Did anyone protest against his actions then? Did anyone bring him to the account he deserved? No, only Holmes saw him for what he was! And we are left to accept this lie, given out publicly behind this colonel's sanctimonious grief!"

"There is one way to combat that," I said, though I know it might cause even more pain. "Why not publish 'The Final Problem'? Why not give your own side of this story, of what Holmes's actual last words and action were? Would that not set the record straight?"

He looked away, quite paralysed by his emotions. "I can't argue with your logic, Mary. That would be the best thing to do." He crumpled as he said it. "Writing it all down, though, bringing up all those emotions I've buried away. It just makes it ... so very final."

16 April—The Moriarty situation has continued to progress. So heated was the reaction to Colonel Moriarty's inflammatory comments that his original letters have been reprinted. Though the Colonel claimed to dislike the public attention these letters attracted, he has not been slow in publicly repeating his allegations. More letters have appeared, and indeed it has provoked quite a flurry of cross-purposed recrimination. Though James and I are heartened that the public support has remained firmly with Sherlock Holmes, James feels that the very existence of these recriminations too greatly besmirches his reputation.

The other day, he went in to meet with Herbert Greenhough Smith and George Newnes at the *Strand* offices. My weakness of constitution from earlier in the year seems to have quite passed me by, so I went into town with James. I received quite a shock, however, when I left him and walked out onto Fleet Street. For there, entering the building as I was departing it, was a familiarly ascetic, dome-headed gentleman.

"Professor Moriarty!" I shrieked. It caused quite a scene on that quiet street. Numerous citizens turned their heads, and a passing constable stopped nearby.

"It's quite all right, Officer," the man replied. "An easy enough mistake. I am Colonel James Moriarty, at your service."

"You are ... uncannily similar to him. If I did not know so certainly he was dead." I could not keep the revulsion from my voice.

"You must be Mrs. Mary Watson, as few people know my brother on sight. I would prefer not to discuss the matter with you, as I am shortly to discuss it with your husband and this penny-dreadful rag that publishes that Sherlock Holmes drivel."

Now that I looked closer at him, I could see they were not the same man. He had a redder face, whose lines and rivets had been carved from the open air of his military service. His head did not quite have the extreme enlargement of the Professor's, and there was no spark of intelligence—or indeed, of madness—in his eyes. He bore instead the face of an unremarkable, unimaginative, but diligent military man. The ruddy tint to his cheeks suggested a propensity for emotional outbursts. I could see the kind of anger that would lead this man to protect his brother's name by destroying that of Sherlock Holmes.

"You will understand, Colonel Moriarty, if I do not wish you well in your meeting," I said and swiftly departed.

Later—James has come to see the only course of action that will satisfy all parties. He must go ahead with publication of 'The Final Problem'. This is of great delight to the *Strand* personnel, who are sure it shall sell well.

"It sounds so ridiculous I know, but part of me had thought by avoiding writing it down, a part of Sherlock Holmes might remain alive—all those readers might still believe it, and there would be something positive, if untrue, in that belief. It will feel like letting him die again—worse, as though I killed him myself this time."

"How could you kill him? Look how his name lives and flourishes, farther and wider than it did in his life. I don't think anyone could kill Holmes, *really* kill him, now even if they wanted to. Not Moriarty, not Arthur Conan Doyle, certainly not you."

21 May—James has finally completed 'The Final Problem'. He has spent more time on its finesse than many of his previous accounts, and the strain of putting these emotional events on paper has begun to show on him. He announced its completion with a desolate, emotionless voice that he often used to conceal when his emotions were at their highest.

31 May—Arthur and I have both read over 'The Final Problem'. I could well see the difficulty James had in its composition, and I in truth find it painful and difficult to read for that reason. He did as excellent a job as he could, though, of capturing that very difficult matter.

I have a feeling that the desperate condition of 'Tooie' has left Arthur less than focussed on his writing. He is not lacking for work—*Sir Nigel, The White Company*, and others are all nearing publication, and I believe in no small part due to the Holmes association he has become a phenomenally admired author on both sides of the Atlantic.

Earlier this year he made a trip around America and was full of praise for it.

It has made him rather callous about Holmes though. Sometimes I think he is as guilty as those *Strand* readers for treating Holmes as though he were a fictional character. How else can I explain his brusque comments regarding 'The Final Problem': "I'm convinced that this is an ideal ending for Sherlock Holmes. After all, I'm sure I wasn't the only one of us feeling a little trapped by the man? Am I right, Dr. Watson? Don't you feel ready to step out of his great looming shadow?"

James was quite speechless. "You … you don't think it might be interesting to publish further memoirs of Sherlock Holmes? There were several cases I never had the chance to reveal to the public, and they would no doubt be interested in them. 'The Second Stain', for instance, or *The Hound of the Baskervilles*—enough material there for a whole novel on its own!"

Arthur saw James's distress and became contrite. "Of course, I didn't mean … I just meant for the time being. Perhaps one day those cases could be published. Maybe those *Strand* readers will grow tired of him, eh?" He laughed, but seeing his badinage was misplaced, he resumed his seriousness. "John, I truly meant no offence. I was speaking of my own writing career, and it was wrong of me to imply that your friend was any kind of burden to me."

Under the circumstances, James understood. He would never hold a grudge against Arthur anyway, and his present adversities are added reason.

In any case, 'The Final Problem' is now in the possession of Herbert Greenhough Smith. He of course, greatly enjoyed it and reiterated how thrilled he would be to publish it. It has rather more sensitive legal implications than previous stories, though, and in order to avoid a civil suit being filed by Colonel Moriarty, he has been advised to delay publication until January of next year.

17 July—My illness, which seemed to have left me for a while, has returned with a vengeance. Having been bed-ridden for a few days now, James has now insisted on a medical examination. He is chiding himself for taking so long at it, but he has been extremely distracted professionally, and in my defence I have concealed my ever-increasing infirmity with expertise.

It seems a trifle perverse to hide symptom when one's husband is a doctor. But as my body seems to lose its lustre daily, there was a deep form of denial at work within me. Is it not always the case, that one hopes that by avoiding an examination, nothing ill can happen? As long as I held off such an appointment, nothing was there to be found and I could pleasantly pretend that nothing would be found.

24 July—James has as yet told me nothing of his findings. He is impossible to read, and has been as open and pleasant with little Mary as usual, even taking some charge of her when I am not sufficiently strong.

The Morstan nature, however, has risen within me again, and I cannot help but fear the worst.

29 July—Still more troubling news, and there is only one inference I can reach from it. James has announced that he thinks it would be better if I were to take another trip to Switzerland.

"I am aware that it is not quite the season yet, but I believe it is … the best thing for you at the present time."

"But James, we have been relatively recently. Are you sure there is no specific reason for it?"

My heart fell when I saw him react with evasion. "Certainly not. I believe Tooie is still there, you can keep her company as she convalesces."

"James, I have a stronger constitution than you are giving me credit. Do not spare my feelings."

His resolve did not last, for he then responded with a long, low howl of tears. I took him in my arms. "My only hope, my dear Mary, is that I am not too late. Arthur berates himself for his shoddy medical skill, and I must do the same. With any luck, though, some time in the Alps should clear out those lungs and get you back to your old self."

24 August—James and I departed for Switzerland today. Mrs. Forrester and little Mary saw us off at the train. The young girl is bearing up incredibly well, and I tried to retain my composure as I said goodbye to her. In truth, I do not know if I shall be well enough to return.

Tomorrow is our anniversary, and I have a grim feeling it will be our last in this world.

(Mary spent most of the autumn convalescing in Switzerland, and presumably corresponded with her husband rather than record her diary. Unfortunately, no record of this correspondence survives, and this unhappy entry is the final one recorded for 1893.)

1894

In some manner he had learned of my own sad bereavement, and his sympathy was shown in his manner rather than in his words. "Work is the best antidote to sorrow, my dear Watson," said he.
— *'The Empty House' (1903)*

2 February—Though it shall do me no good, I have decided to return to England. I would rather be surrounded by James and little Mary, and my familiar life, as I end my days, no matter how much pain I may have to tolerate.

My time in Switzerland has not been wasted. I feel up to something approaching my earlier health, certainly better than I have felt for quite a while. However, my condition is simply too advanced, and there is nothing that can be done but to be sanguine about the grim possibilities that lie ahead for me.

My family was far too solicitous of my health, and I repeatedly told James I wanted him to be just as he always is, and not to think me too delicate to talk and act normally. Little Mary has been her usual brave self in the face of this.

'The Final Problem' finally saw print in the *Strand*. Its editors have had cause to rue its publication, James noted with some satisfaction. For upon reading that Sherlock Holmes was dead, 20,000 subscribers cancelled their subscriptions in outrage! When I disembarked from the train, I idly commented that I had seen a great many gentlemen at the station wearing black armbands. Still more were walking the streets of London so attired, that I guessed Prime Minister Gladstone must have passed away.

"Not at all, Mary," James said with a curious satisfaction. At this moment I saw that he too had one tied around his arm. "It is for Sherlock Holmes! I cannot quite believe it, but the outpouring of support at learning of his death … you were certainly right for persuading me to publish it my dear. More than that—you were right that he could not be killed by my account of his death, if that makes sense."

"If I was right, then of course it makes sense."

13 February—The past few weeks have seen more than a few visitors to our house wishing to spend time with me and share their condolences. It has been refreshing, if eventually exhausting, to see so many friends *en masse*. Some I have not visited with since our wedding. Others—like Kate and Mrs. Forrester—are regular friends whose company is always cherishable. Kate, indeed, was a pleasure to see, as she is a much freer and gayer woman than she has been for several years.

This encounter recalls to me something James had mentioned.

"It was towards the close of last year. I was out on my rounds, which had taken me all the way down to Southwark. So well had the day progressed, and so close was I, that my mind had begun to wander to the prospect of a post-work trip to Camberwell to see little Mary and Mrs. Forrester. I was contemplating this prospect when a voice called out to me:

" 'Doctor Watson! Doctor John Watson!' it trilled. I turned around to see a familiar bald-headed man, dressed in an extravagantly dandified brocaded velvet coat. It was none other than Thaddeus Sholto.

" 'Mr. Sholto,' I rejoined. 'Good God, how exceedingly odd to run across you after all this time!'

"Though my impressions of Sholto from five years ago had been coloured by his mannered behaviour, I had in truth been so preoccupied with my work and your absence that I had talked to few people in a non-professional capacity. I greeted him, thus, with more warmth than would otherwise have been the case.

"For a while we talked of his activities for the last few years. In this time, I quickly came to regret my initial sociability, but found myself trapped in the conversation and unable to extricate myself."

"How very like you, dear James," I smiled. "Your manners are so often your undoing."

"They were sorely tested on this occasion, I can tell you my dear. I cannot recall a more self-absorbed and self-pitying litany than the one he then laid upon me. The absence of his brother had only exacerbated his unfortunate eccentricities, and it seemed he had found no useful outlet for his energies. He mostly continued as he had done before, collecting art and travelling, and generally frittering away the money he had, while pining uselessly after the money he could have had from the Agra treasure.

" 'How differently my life would have gone, I assure you!' he insisted. 'I would not be stuck in these straitened circumstances, and would certainly have left London for more exotic shores. It is a shame to have devoted one's life to such a promise and find, in its absence, nothing of greater stimulation. That is my tragedy, and at the age of thirty-and-six now, any opportunities have truly passed me by.'

" 'Nonsense, Mr. Sholto!' I declared. 'There are only such opportunities in this world as you can make for yourself.'

"He regarded my words with an unspoken condescension and, more out of a feigned politeness than genuine manners, he turned the conversation to my own affairs of the last few years.

" 'I recall reading of your wedding to that charming Miss Morstan,' he said. 'Do you know, had matters turned out differently, I do often wonder if I could have been a marriageable prospect for that young lady!'

" 'It was my good fortune that you were not,' I replied coolly.

" 'Ah, but your prospects would have been considerably more distant had my treasure not sunk to the bottom of the Thames. I sometimes wonder whether I could purchase diving gear and recover it myself. Hmm, something to look into, I suppose. Anyway, I must be off—

184

give my regards to Mr. Holmes.' He had left before the hurt of the *faux pas* had sunk in.

"The encounter had somewhat lowered my spirits as I made my way to Camberwell, and I turned my thoughts to Sholto's alternative chain. What if you had recovered that treasure? What if you were Mrs. Mary Sholto? Even if you did not have the treasure, you may have been happier. You may not have been condemned to this … this state."

While I was first inclined to take his thoughts as comical, I realized his fancy had a tone of wistful regret. "You cannot be serious!" I cried.

"He may not have been an ideal match, but who knows? Perhaps your misfortune is my fault."

"James what stuff and nonsense you are talking! Thaddeus Sholto indeed! I could indeed have married him—and died shortly after by being hit by a coach and pair. Or we could have murdered each other, having been slowly driven mad—or in his case, madder. Even if I had lived to a hundred with Thaddeus and the Agra treasure, I know for a fact that nothing in that life could have given me the riches I have in you. Think, for instance, of little Mary."

"Hum, I am glad to hear you say that, even if you are bound to as my wife."

"Ha, not necessarily."

9 March—How frustrating it is, to find my energy diminishing daily but so much to do, and to write down! I often feel bloody-minded perseverance, and the ever-growing list of obligations I must discharge before I am able to truly rest in peace, are all that are staving off my increasingly inevitable fate.

Mrs. Forrester has paid me a visit, and said she wished to discuss something with little Mary and myself. "I hope I can be of assistance to you, Mary," she said, "and having looked after young Mary while you were away, I believe it might be best if I were to take over as her guardian in the vent of … anything untoward happening."

She then asked that little Mary come in, and my daughter was very well-spoken in her wishes, which were that she go into Mrs. Forrester's care.

'Would you not miss your father, though, Mary?" I asked her.

"Well, of course I would," she answered. "But it's so difficult for him even as it is."

"You certainly are as self-effacing as your mother, Mary," Mrs. Forrester told the young girl. So that she would not be too distressed, I asked that Mrs. Forrester talk with me alone.

"I'd worry about Mary if Dr. Watson was looking after her," she confessed. "He has been so distracted of late, and I don't think he'd have the necessary commitment to his daughter. You should consider yourself lucky that I'm not going anywhere just yet…" A few tears rolled down her cheek as she said this. "Oh, I can't believe you've gotten so terribly ill! Isn't there anything Watson can do about this?"

"My husband has done all he could. Truthfully, I am more concerned about him than about myself. He does depend on me rather a lot."

"I don't doubt that," Mrs. Forrester ejaculated through her sobs.

"Please, Mrs. Forrester, you don't need to get so emotional on my behalf. I feel calm in an odd way about my fate. Especially now that I know Mary shall be so well looked after in your charge. Just as I was."

Strange though it may seem, I did feel a kind of serenity at this. My own fate has seldom concerned me less now that it is so irredeemably doomed. However, I cannot consider myself truly lost while I know that those I love most shall be looked after. If I could only find someone to give James similar attention and care...

But setting him up with a new wife is a little beyond my means, even were I at my best!

4 April—I count myself lucky that James has many subjects that naturally interest him, and as his wife, they interest me to hear him talk of them.

Even these years later, any hint of crime or malfeasance in the papers will fire his curiosity. In this way, the spirit of Holmes remains very alive in him, though I know he has, more fully than ever, come to terms with his death. In some ways, seeing me so close to the next realm has perhaps made the reality of his earlier bereavement sink in.

But anyhow, he is much occupied with the details of this latest disquiet in the most polite corners of London society. The details are as vexing as any Sherlock Holmes would have been faced with.

The Honourable Ronald Adair, a former Australian governor, had returned to London and had become quite well known in the society circles of Park Lane. He was a keen card player. On the evening of March 30, he had returned from a game alone, and when his mother and sister returned from their evening out, they found him dead in the sitting room. The door was locked from the inside, and beside two bank notes for £10 each and piles of silver and gold to the tune of £10 17s., lay a sheet of paper with the names of his friends at the club written on it. One could be forgiven for thinking he had taken his own life at the prospect of working out his debts to his fellow gamblers, but there was no weapon in the room, and the window outside had a twenty-foot drop. Most gruesomely, the bullet used to deal the mortal blow was an expanding revolver bullet—a monstrously savage touch.

There were additional, puzzling quirks that had no doubt attracted James to this intrigue. A few weeks earlier he had won £420 from Lord Balmoral, whose association with Holmes had procured us that charming room in Park Lane for our wedding. Even stranger, both that night and on the night of his death, among his fellow card players at the Bagatelle Club was one Colonel Moran. Though the Colonel's Christian name was not recorded in the report, James had reason to believe it was the same Moran who spoke in Professor Moriarty's defence in his brother's poison pen letter of last year.

James admitted to me that reading over the police inquest had given him greater absorption than any of his patients had of late.

"You remain a detective first, a writer second, and a doctor third," I chided him. "As my present condition attests."

"My dear Mary, you should not joke about such things."

"I am still alive, and with you, so I cannot help but think myself lucky," I said frankly.

7 April—I grow steadily weaker, and feel certain that death cannot be far away. I have fought against it with every fibre of my being, but know I can hold it back no more.

I am so desperately afraid! Not for myself—the spectre of death has perhaps been so familiar throughout my life that it held little fear for me.

No, I fear for my sweet, beloved James. James has been fragile enough these past three years, and with no modesty I say that I have been partly responsible for maintaining his condition. There is so much he cannot cope with on his own—why, why must Fate have twisted its knife so cruelly into the back of one who so embodied decency!

11 April—Sometimes everyday life, having cruelly eroded hope for so long, will then greedily bestow miracles in compensation! Today, as my candle flickers to its last embers, I feel at peace. Indeed, I feel better than that—more whole than I have for many months. I hope I can muster enough strength to write the two incredible encounters that make my hopes so solid.

The day began as darkly as ever—I cannot recall even the notoriously gloomy London having such grey, oppressive weather for quite this long in all my years. I felt even worse than I have the previous few days, and my consumption seemed so acute that at any moment I felt the Grim Reaper would knock on my door.

These feelings were amplified whenever the nurse left the room. In this case, she had merely gone to get a sandwich for herself and a cup of tea for me, but as soon as the door shut and I was alone, I felt the darkness close in more acutely.

When a visitor did arrive, he was not admitted through the front door. In fact, seeing the figure jemmy the high window open and slither through it in a most lithe manner, I was certain I was in some ghastly reverie. This feeling did not dissipate when the man turned to me, and I saw he was a shabbily attired bookseller. Ordinarily I would have called for someone to help, but at that moment I looked deeply into his eyes, and the familiarity in them caused me nearly to lose my senses.

But the hope—the hope that recognition engendered—it made me struggle to cling on for as long as humanly possible. For you see... the bookseller was none other than Sherlock Holmes!

"Mrs. Watson, do not be alarmed," he wheezed in an affected high voice.

"Mister ... Holmes ..." I wheezed out with all the energy I could.

He cast his eyes skyward, for a moment more irritated that I had seen through another disguise than what he had come to say. But he controlled himself, removed the false beard that was practically *de rigeur* in these get-ups, and pulled a chair to my bedside.

"Mrs. Watson, how long do you suppose?"

"Not long ..."

For the first time in my entire acquaintanceship with Holmes, he stood speechless before me. "To see you like this ... this fills me with grief." He said this without emotion, but I chose to believe he meant it.

"To see you alive ... fills me with a commensurate joy. How on earth did you survive?"

"A trifling matter—all to do with the Japanese martial art of *bartitsu*, which allowed me to control my breathing underwater ... but please, never mind me. How are you?"

"I have been quite dire, Mr. Holmes. These last years have steadily worn me down, eroded my spirit as much or more than my body. And James has been worse, without you."

"I perceive you are angry with me."

It was such a bluntly obtuse statement that for a moment I contemplated responding with the coarse expression using his name that was common on the London streets[13]. Instead I rejoined with a withering, "What an extraordinary deduction. I sincerely hope you have an explanation for concealing your survival from James."

"It was Moriarty. His organization still had some active tentacles. I thought that having severed the head, they would die in due course, but they continued to thrash independently. For Watson's safety I could not reveal anything to him. I was concerned for him … and also for you and your charming daughter."

"You cannot know how low your absence has laid him. The anguish it has provoked."

"I should be gratified to hear that. But please accept my assurance that it was vital."

"Why then, have you returned to London? Is it now safe?"

Holmes vibrated with cynical laughter. "I should wager less than ever. Moriarty's chief of staff, Colonel Sebastian Moran, roams the London streets plotting my assassination. You may have read of the death of the Honourable Ronald Adair—his handiwork. However, I am ready for him, and I have a deception that he shall never suspect."

The energy with which Holmes related his exotic deeds and what lay in store filled me with a similar animation. More than that, I was overcome with joy—joy

---

[13] Most scholars believe this was some Victorian predecessor to the modern-day coarse expression, "No sh*t, Sherlock." No one, however, can find specific examples of what the phrase would have been, and its modern variant apparently first appears in 1970s New York slang.

that there was something beyond the grey slate of the London sky, beyond my deteriorating health, beyond the certainties of the lengthy and enervating death that seemed my lot. I told Holmes as much—no doubt seeming very sentimental and inelegant.

He, however, was a changed man since last I had seen him. The sharpness, acidity, and inhumanity seemed to have left him as he sat by my side and listened to my rambling account of the last two years. He was solicitous and sympathetic. There should be nothing surprising about that—who else but Holmes could return from that undiscovered country I am bound so shortly for?

Our talk was all too quickly cut short by the nurse traipsing up the steps. "I do wonder what could have kept her, enjoyable though I have found this discussion?"

Holmes gave a perfunctory check of his pocket watch. "The water will only have switched back on about five minutes, twenty-six seconds ago, so she has performed her tasks admirably with that … unanticipated handicap."

I laughed at his effrontery. "Something, of course, you would know nothing about?" I asked.

"Modesty forbids me to say."

"Now I doubt you really are Sherlock Holmes. He possessed no modesty."

The maid was now trying the door, which Holmes's pile of books appeared to have stopped. "I expect I shall not see you again, Mrs. Watson. Let me tell you again how sad I am—if I could prolong your own life by even one day at the cost of my own, I would gladly do it."

"And I you," I replied with full candour. "You see, I was so desperately worried about James without you *and* myself in his life. But now that I know … I know that you will be returning to his side … as long as his future is happy, then mine is also."

Without another word, Holmes climbed to the window, and pulled his books up by their length of string. The door now unloosed, the maid came crashing in just as he disappeared down the side of our house.

"Something had stuck that there door," she explained. "By the way, Doctor Watson has sent a telegram that he would be on his way directly."

I shall keep my strength up—hold death's door back, as much as I can—by writing down this extraordinary experience, while I wait for my dear James to return. Oh, how I hope that I can look upon his face one more time! To know that there is someone in this miserable world to look after him, someone with whom his *joie de vivre* can return! It makes me feel so wonderfully light, I almost feel quite well again!

By the time James arrived, my energy had dissipated. "I don't know who sent me the telegram, the maid says she knows nothing about it," he mumbled.

"It doesn't matter," I answered, not wanting to ruin the surprise that lay in store for him. "Please, James, do look after yourself. And make sure little Mary is cared for by Mrs. Forrester."

"I shall see to her care myself," he said.

"I think you may find yourself otherwise occupied," I admitted coyly. James of course thought I was delirious, but I had to say one more thing to him. "By the way … I think it would do you good to look out for a bookseller …"

"A bookseller? What do you mean?"

"Just one of those street vendors with the little bundles of books. You never know who you might run into selling books."

"Of course I shall. If you say so, dear."

I wrote up these last few words, but now I must put my pen down for the last time. I have spent my last moments so very happy. I am so happy for the reunion that lies in store for James. I am happy that he has been here by my side. Ultimately, I shall end my days in happiness. And that is all anyone can ask at the end of their life.

1895-1926

*The good Watson had at that time deserted me for a wife,
the only selfish action which I can recall in our association.
I was alone.*
— *'The Blanched Soldier' (1926)*

(*The following is an abridgement of Mary Forrester's
recordings.*)

I was not present when my mother passed away, and
over the following years I grew to feel I had not been
present when she was alive. For not only was she, who was
more dear to me than anyone else in my life, now gone. But
my father, who had been so caring and solicitous a parent in
my dimly-remembered toddling years, changed completely.

It was not long after Mother's funeral that the
formal process of Mrs. Forrester's custody over me was
committed to paper. For the purposes of schooling, I was
registered as Mary Victoria Watson Forrester, and it was as
a Forrester that, most days, I came to identify myself.

Mrs. Forrester was as loving and supportive to me
as she had been to my mother. Some women have a
naturally maternal nature, and it seems so cruel that she was
never blessed with children of her own. I cannot imagine
any child who would not benefit from the tutelage and
encouragement of someone like her.

196

I spent several years feeling, in my marrow, to be a little emptier from Mother's absence. Any more personal feelings, I held back with every fibre of my being. With a few years' distance I had dulled the sharp sensations, and the painful memories, of those early months of 1894, and focussed almost entirely on the trivialities of the present: my school and my ambitions in adulthood. To a child, the passage of a few years can be such a wide gulf that I had detached myself from those desperately sad memories of my dear mother's last days.

My exception to this was visiting, once or twice a week, Mother's graveside. I made sure, though, to contain what I had felt there, and as such it felt like a spiritual separation from my daily routine.

I had, of course, been complicit in the arrangement in which I grew up. However, in my childish naïveté I had not thought it would be as great a wrench to me as it undoubtedly was. I cannot say I bore my father ill will for this. The years may have hurt me as they passed, but I never directed what anger and heartbreak I felt at anyone—least of all a man I regarded with such love.

I fully remember that day in April when he told me of Sherlock Holmes's return. "I knew he'd be all right," I said with my youthful arrogance.

"Of course you did, my dear. Why do I not always listen to you and your mother, eh? But it's the most important secret, you know. You cannot tell anyone that he is alive. It's the most important thing you can do. Just between ourselves, eh?"

197

I was happy then to be taken into his confidence.

The most important question to me as I think back on this time was: at what point did I know my father was beginning a new life—a life without me? Frustratingly to me now, I find this a very difficult question to answer. There was no definitive moment, no point of no return. There was just a slow accretion of details and disappointments that drove my father and me further apart.

I attended his wedding in 1902, along with Mrs. Forrester and a few of Father's friends, then only dimly familiar to me. Sherlock Holmes still wished the public to think him dead, so he attended in disguise—wearing an elaborate moustache, darkening his skin to give him a faintly Mediterranean appearance, and adding some particularly obvious false jowls. He was introduced to all the guests as Mr. Altamont, a friend of Father's from the club. I, however, saw through him at once—a talent I had evinced even as a little girl. Sometimes I think Holmes himself tipped me the wink, as it were, because there was always something about his eyes that gave his true self away—a certain kindliness that he would probably not bestow upon a criminal. With his secret safe, he took on an avuncular interest in my school-work, and we talked at length over the wedding breakfast. I remember being quite embarrassed when Mr. Holmes reminded me that in my youth, I had such difficulty pronouncing his name.

Perhaps I was being naïve, but I really had no inkling that his new wife would change Father so thoroughly. Holmes was as terse with her as he was with most people (I noted with some pride that I marked an exception to his aversion of the fair sex, no doubt aided by the affection he held for my mother). She was a younger woman, her accent carried with it a trace of American pronunciation. Like many Americans, she was gregarious and warm, but I think now that there was insincerity behind her kind words.

"Don't you look lovely!" she said to me. I was, at a precocious twelve years of age, slightly too old to take such compliments at their face value, and became embarrassed at the attention. As we talked, she said, "Mrs. Forrester is doing such a splendid job bringing you up. I am so glad to have you in our family."

"I am glad also," I replied with as much propriety as I could manage.

Nevertheless, I took from this exchange a promise that I would return to my father soon. It is an odd trick of the mind that I did so, as I now think back on the conversation and see that this was patently not what was said.

This promise remained unfulfilled over the months to come. During that time I felt more anger and disappointment towards my new stepmother than Father, but I actually thought little of it. Perhaps it was some mark of denial on my part that I latched quite so voraciously on to the fresh *Sherlock Holmes* stories published by Sir Arthur Conan Doyle in the new century. This new avenue opened up to me one day after school, when I came upon the then-recently published *The Hound of the Baskervilles* at a small shop on Charing Cross Road. It was commonly believed that Sir Arthur's knighthood had came about because he bowed to public demand and 'resurrected' Sherlock Holmes (though I remained smug in my knowledge that he was still alive), and I shared the nation's gratitude entirely.

I read the whole book in one sitting—and was thrilled to think that this dark and supernatural tale, with its elements of folklore and adventure, and its exotic wilderness setting of Dartmoor, was actually solved and experienced by these two men whom I considered my nearest kin. That strange disjunction—of not quite being able to believe the reality of these accounts—was a sensation that I recall fondly from reading it. For what did seem real, and indeed I knew and remembered from just a few years earlier, was the robust dependability of my dear father. I pored over his words and actions as much as Holmes's—and I was so pleased that he had such a prominent role in the story, making the initial investigations of Baskerville Hall and protecting Sir Henry, while Holmes observed from afar.

As soon as I had finished the book, I went back and re-read it from the beginning. Its uncanny power and lustre seemed to gain with the second reading, and this time I paid more attention to details and embellishments that had first escaped me. It was not the simple family connection, but a genuine love of the thrilling and adventurous tale Father had told, that I found so compelling and fascinating.

Following this, I went back and discovered the *Adventures* and *Memoirs* of Sherlock Holmes, and after that the earliest novels, *A Study in Scarlet* and *The Sign of Four*. I cannot recall how often I have re-read these books. Some lines are as familiar and precious to me as Shakespeare or Scripture passages. I know from Mother's diary that Conan Doyle was sceptical and dismissive of the 'fans' Holmes had attracted. I know that my father regarded his hostility towards the Holmes character as more than a little mean-spirited, and I somewhat resented it as well. However, I was just glad, glad to be in the company once more of this great family that I had become detached from.

Though as a student and a scholar of Father's writing and Holmes's celebrated detective methods I admired various qualities in many different episodes, my favourite was always *The Sign of Four*. There was something so very romantic about it—even though Father showed considerable restraint in describing Mother—and having such a frank and candid account of their first meeting constantly reminded me of the love they held for each other. It was a love I was confident was still very present when Mother breathed her last. Whether it was Father's relation or Conan Doyle's presentation, the story's concluding chapter was magically poignant for me. The personal connection it held, and the distance it showed between the two men, and the promise of the happy life Father then believed lay long ahead for himself and

Mother—considering all that made me, for the first time, lose my composure and confront the sorrow that for so long lay numbing my heart.

Fresh from this strange self-discovery—and perhaps right in the crux of the confusing emotions that many girls feel in their thirteenth year—I reacted perhaps slightly badly to Mrs. Forrester's confrontation with me over my choice of reading material. She tore *The Sign of Four* out of my hand and gripped it so tightly I thought she was going to snap its spine in two.

"John Watson!" she spat.

"Whatever is the matter, Mrs. Forrester?" I asked innocently.

"That man! Seeing his name fills me with such anger!" she roared.

Knowing Mrs. Forrester's placid temperament, I was surprised at this anger. Her worst character trait until now had been a certain eagerness to judge, but this was an entirely new and unexpected facet. Additionally, it was confusing as only a few weeks earlier we were both guests at Father's wedding, and she was perfectly cordial to him and his new wife—my stepmother, it seems odd to record.

It seemed as though the redder passions that I was in the throes of were mirrored and amplified by the elder woman's.

"Mrs. Forrester, whatever has come over you?" I asked, slightly unsettled in truth by all this lack of composure. "What has Father done to deserve such hostility?"

"What has your father done indeed? Mary, I can't believe you can ask that question! Seeing him go off with another woman as though he were ... buying a new hat!"

"You disapprove of his new wife?"

"I disapprove, you silly child, of the whole union! Surely you must be emotional about it yourself? To think of your poor mother ... taken so young! At least my Cecil had led a full life when ... when!" She stopped talking and angrily waved her hand in my face. I could see from the beady squint she was giving me that the memories were extremely painful for her. "Perhaps you don't understand."

It seems bloodless of me, and not a little cruel, but at that moment I felt angry at her insensitivity to my sadness. With the passage of time, I can see she saw in me a lack of empathy for her own deep wells of sorrow, but I did not draw this connection. As a result, my response to her was high-handed and a little cold.

"Our grief takes different forms, Mrs. Forrester. For instance, it is through reading my father's accounts of his early, happy days with Mother, that I for the first time properly considered her terrible absence from my life. I hope you can appreciate that."

She nodded acquiescently, and uttered a slightly mumbled apology. "It just all seems such a waste. To think that there's nothing that can be done anymore. To think how he's let you down as a father."

"But surely, he has seen to my education and my upbringing."

"Financially, yes, he has. And very grateful I am for that, and I think it is sweet of you to accept it for what it is. But he has remained so absent, so distant. I don't know how he can treat you that way."

"I think it's unfair of you to judge him by such … prosaic markers," I said haughtily. "He is, after all, not merely concerned with his living and his family. He plays for so much larger stakes. It would be selfish of me to demand more commitment from him! Read his writing, Mrs. Forrester, recall your own part in it … then you will see why we are lucky to even have the fleeting contact we did with my father."

Mrs. Forrester flipped through the book. I really hoped she would take it and read it, but she seemed to use it more as an *aide-memoire* for her recollections. At the time I thought her a little self-centred to do so, but as an adult I see why she did so.

"Things were so different then, but now … just a few years later, and we're all so alone. Him, of course, by choice. But to cut off his own daughter like he's done. At first I regarded him and Holmes as good people, their eccentricities endearing. To see Mary—your mother—at the time, well I had never seen her so happy."

"I know, Mrs. Forrester. Father recalls it with the same happiness. You can read it all in here."

With some trepidation, I slid the now discarded George Newnes hardback her way. She flipped through it cursorily—registering a tiny smirk at the illustrations that gave Holmes a beard or a moustache—but then she dropped the book on the table.

"You are very right, dear Mary. I cannot begrudge you this connection. But I cannot revisit it, there's nothing but pain in there for me now. All that was happy and bright about those days is now withered and blighted."

Not being able to talk my thoughts over with Mrs. Forrester, and having no one at school who remotely understood any of these complexities, I turned Mother's life over in my mind, repeatedly. I cast my mind back to her last years of life so I could absorb their every detail. There seems to me now, writing this down, something of hero-worship about all this, as I was using the methods of Holmes to detach myself from my emotions and collect an ample and unabridged mental encyclopaedia of this turmoil. Perhaps then, I could understand it.

Whatever my reasoning, I pored over these details. I recalled how deeply Father had mourned her, and how empty his life seemed without her and Holmes. I intimately knew and felt his fragility, his need for support. In some ways, he was more vulnerable than Mother in that regard. A quiet stoicism had entered into her early, from her lifelong isolation and her travelling. Perhaps it concealed sadness and regret, but it gave the impression of a strong constitution in its own way. Father was never a solitary man, enjoying the company of fellow soldiers, of the gentlemen at his club and his old school friends, and lastly and most importantly, of Sherlock Holmes.

Anyhow, I tried to convey some of the impressions I now write down to Mrs. Forrester. My lack of consideration made them inevitably sound a trifle less formed, and I regret to say I lost my temper with my guardian on several occasions. In her capacity as a governess, she was used to the passions of her pupils, though, and bore my repeated frustrations with patience. I am glad that she did, for it would have caused me great sorrow to lose her wisdom early on owing to my callow lack of understanding.

It is surreal to recall my next encounter with my father was seeing him as a character in a stage melodrama. A friend of mine from school, Constance Quinn, invited me to see William Gillette's *Sherlock Holmes*. I knew that Mrs. Forrester would not approve, so I told her I was attending George Dance's dreary musical, *A Chinese Honeymoon*, playing at the Royal Strand (which, by the way, entailed a side-trip down to Wych Street to pinch a discarded programme in order to complete the deception!).

It seemed a very surreal mix of fact and fiction that *Sherlock Holmes* was playing at the Lyceum Theatre, where fifteen years earlier my mother had her rendezvous with Holmes and Watson and went to Thaddeus Sholto's house.

Just as with *The Hound of the Baskervilles*, I was struck by the closeness and yet the distortion of my kin, as seen through the lens of William Gillette's writing and performance. His Holmes was not the man I knew. And yet he was. That was the true strange power of the distortion, that it still reflected so much that was true in the man. For Holmes was no man of action, did not have women swooning over him, did not have the charisma William Gillette imbued him with. By heaven, Mr. Gillette even spoke in the swaggering tones of an American, not the cultivated and undemonstrative English diction that so soothed me as a younger girl. But behind that—well, 'inaccuracy', dare I say—all of these things *were* true about Holmes.

As I saw this foolish hero, leaping about the stage, escaping from Moriarty's evil clutches, and making declamations of love in the arms of Alice Faulker, I wondered whether I had slightly fallen in love with Sherlock Holmes. I also wondered, comparing the heroic but false stage protagonist with his truer but more alien real-life counterpart, whether this was not sadder and more impossible than any of the improbable melodrama that Mr. Gillette's scenario had inflicted upon theatre-goers.

Constance's mother was principally interested in Mr. Gillette, and perhaps less for his fidelity to the man and myth of Holmes than for his aesthetic qualities. To such fickle but enthusiastic criticism, I know the play measured up most favourably, for both Mrs. Quinn and the audience at large. The large crowd laughed, cheered, and yelled in a manner most unlike the polite and staid London theatre-goers' normal mien. And, when there was widespread laughter and applause at Gillette's invented catch-phrase "Elementary, my dear Watson.", I knew that the audience shared Mrs. Quinn's fascination. I remember feeling somewhat—was it embarrassed? No, surely even that would be unfair of me—but I certainly felt distant when Mrs. Quinn ejaculated a loud sigh at the moment Holmes admitted his life for Alice.

It was this moment that I took issue with as the curtain fell.

"There is nothing in the stories that would suggest Holmes would ever fall in love so glibly. And his words were so out of character, so incredibly false. 'I suppose—indeed I know—that I love you. I love you. But I know as well what I am—and what you are—I know that no such person as I should ever dream of being a part of your sweet life. It would be a crime for me to think of such a thing. There is every reason—'"

"My dear Mary," Mrs. Quinn reproached me. "It is not what Mr. Holmes said, but what Alice did after that."

"She did nothing," I recalled. "In fact, she silenced Holmes before he could explain his reasons, reasons that we loyal fans and readers know he holds above all other things. What a betrayal of Holmes's beliefs!"

"But she held him in her arms. It is not something you, as a girl, would know." She emitted another sigh at this point. I had Holmes's very words from *The Sign of Four*—ending with "I shall never marry myself, lest I bias my judgement"—ready to cite as evidence. However, I realized there was no point reasoning with Mrs. Quinn, gripped as she was by sentiment.

I ended the evening frustrated. I was frustrated that my knowledge of Sherlock Holmes could be neither revealed, nor given the respect it deserved. Instead I was treated like a misunderstanding juvenile. Secondly, there was a touch of—I can think of no other word to call it—a touch of jealousy in my marrow. This Holmes may have been an impostor, but he was still Holmes. I resented having to share him with so many people, I resented the notion that a flibbertigibbet like Alice Faulkner would be a fitting match for him, and I resented people who ill understood talking of him as they would of Lillie Langtry or Herbert Beerbohm Tree. How dare they!

When we talked of it another time, I told Constance what I had thought, no doubt in an inarticulate and silly-sounding way. She laughed and said, "To think, Mary, that I always find you such a serious person!"

"What is that supposed to mean?"

"Well, and here you are nursing some fancy for Sherlock Holmes of all people!"

Constance's plain-talking assessment, paradoxically, cheered me immensely. Indeed, we would often laugh about it and any time I would express a similar sentiment, or she would discuss a boy admirer of hers, she would ruefully mention my fancy. "I know he's no Sherlock Holmes," she might add.

I gave no more serious thought, quite deliberately, of this impossible romantic delusion of mine, which I now deemed could have no bearing on my emotions anyway.

I came of age with many academic achievements to my name. Mrs. Forrester made no secret that she thought that I, like Mother, would make an excellent governess and she would take me on. By this stage, she had grown somewhat enfeebled and had retired, but was on good terms with the current proprietress.

At this time, though—and it somewhat makes me blush to record it—but I had aimed to become a detective myself. Frankly, I could think of no one more equipped to follow in Holmes's footsteps than myself. By this time there was no need to conceal my knowledge of Holmes's survival, as *The Return of Sherlock Holmes* had begun its *Strand* serialization, and begun with the Great Detective's miraculous return from the dead in 'The Empty House'. The stories that followed only strengthened my resolve to learn the science of deduction for myself.

I was now firmly in awe of Holmes, and it was he rather than Watson whom I identified myself with. After all, Holmes who was the master detective—Watson, for all his achievements, was no more than a friendly bystander, a faithful ally but one whose lack of ratiocination became more and more marked. Unlike Watson, who never ceased to be surprised at Holmes's disguises and never attempted to work out his deductions for himself, I would be a protégé who could, one day, rival the mentor. And anyway, why should I aspire to be the conductor of light, not in itself luminous, when I could be the light itself?

It was shortly before my nineteenth birthday that, determined in my resolution but finding no one who could offer me help or advice for it, I decided to visit Holmes and ask him about it. Baker Street had lost none of its tourist allure, and that otherwise unremarkable end of it thronged as usual with passers-by who stopped by its door just long enough to mark out their fervour. It had been devotional enough in 1893, but the passing decades had made it a sort of Mecca for detective 'fans'.

I marched past them and rang the doorbell. I felt like the prodigal son returning to a long-vacated manor seat. I had my argument all worked out, and felt sure I could state my case well enough even for a misogynist of Holmes's standing to see that I was well equipped for the challenge.

I was somewhat knocked back when the door was answered not by the expected Mrs. Hudson, but by an imperious woman in her middle thirties. She took a disdainful survey at the other sightseers assembled outside the door, and no doubt thought my eager expression was simply an outgrowth of theirs. "I must ask you to keep the street clear, please," she replied wearily.

"I'm not with these other people," I explained, trying to set myself apart but also not to judge the poor unfortunates whose only crime was a passion for the character, a passion that I understood and shared. "I am here to ask for an interview with Mr. Holmes."

"You really should have written ahead," she returned. "Or telephoned."

"I was informed by Scotland Yard that Mr. Holmes had his telephone removed."

With a bitterly sardonic smile, she retorted, "That is why you should have telephoned."

"I am certain Mr. Holmes will see me," I quickly interjected, feeling the frosty lady was readying the door to slam into my face. "You see ... I am Mary Watson, his friend and colleague's daughter."

"That is hardly original," she sighed.

I had thought of this, and so pulled from my bag a treasured, but rather crumpled, family photograph taken in Switzerland. There I stood, as a little girl, standing proudly alongside my parents. "You can also make out Arthur Conan Doyle in the corner of the picture."

The woman looked up at me, squinting, before taking the point.

"I recognize the eyes." She looked around at the citizens, who were now even more interested by this new development and drew nearer to the door to overhear. One person in particular—a drably attired man in his late twenties, whose inquisitive gaze told me he had 'dressed down' for the purposes of observing Baker Street without himself being observed—stayed in my mind.

"We cannot really talk out here," the maid said frankly. "Why don't you come inside?"

This was my first visit to Baker Street, and as with Gillette's play, there was a sense of dislocation in seeing a life-like representation of something that formerly existed—but existed so vividly—in my mind. Perversely, I found the decay that spread across the whole environment added to its appeal: that distinctive furniture Father described so specifically was crumbling, the mantelpiece had a dent in it from years of correspondence fixed to it with a jack-knife. The far wall decorated with its 'V.R.' in bullet-holes had been repainted (which did not hide the blemishes), and the smell was a pungently fusty mixture of years of smoke and dust.

Yet it was not the dilapidation but the emptiness that most affected me. There was no jack-knife, a few letters lay neatly piled upon the table, the shelves were largely devoid of books, and the surfaces were polished. The sight of this cleanliness, clearly unnatural in this space, put me on edge.

The whole experience was simultaneously prosaic and unreal. I walked around the rooms in silence for longer than the maid, certainly, expected.

"Where is Mrs. Hudson?" I asked, still awed by my surroundings. "Will Mr. Holmes be out for long?"

I sat down in a basket chair, whose ancient arm buckled from my pressure, and the maid—who introduced herself as Martha—stood by the fire. This resulted in her awkwardly looming over me throughout our interview. She was clearly uncomfortable at the posture yet too self-conscious to take a seat herself.

"I am afraid I won't be able to help you, and that you won't be able to see Mr. Holmes. I'm very sorry."

"I could return another time."

"No, you don't understand. Mr. Holmes retired last year."

"I see. I appreciate that he would not want to be disturbed, but I only came hear to ask for his endorsement in a professional matter."

"And you say you are Dr. Watson's daughter?"

"I don't need to say it. You saw the photograph."

This brought out some softness in Martha's hard-lined features. But it was only for a moment, and then her placidly stony expression resumed. "I do not know where he could be found. He needs some disconnection from the outside world. The strain of his work got to him in the end, you understand."

"I see," I replied. "In that case, I will say good day to you. I can't see the point of staying if Mr. Holmes is unwilling—"

"Unable, surely," Martha corrected me.

"The result is the same. I can't count on his help," I concluded, pushing past her and leaving the house.

Dejected by this turn of events, I ultimately relied on Father's machinations to gain me admission to St. Hilda's, Oxford (then the newest women's college). I had long been sceptical about the disadvantages a woman faced studying there. However, the year before I began my studies, the university buzzed with the furore over the 'Steamboat Ladies'[14]. Their example emboldened me to the possibilities of women's education and like them, I was able to receive an *ad eundem* degree also.

---

[14] Between the years 1904 and 1907, students at the female colleges in Oxford and Cambridge were granted *ad eundem* degrees (degrees of the same rank conferred by a different university) from Trinity College, Dublin. They were so called because they took steamboats to Dublin for this purpose.

I definitively adopted the surname of Forrester at this time, as my family connection was a particularly delicate matter here. For it was in these dreaming spires that the study of Sherlock Holmes became a formal, but no less fanatical, discipline. A student a year older than me, one Ronald Knox, was studying Classics, and his hobby and enthusiasm for Sherlock Holmes was well-known. As I am sure most Holmes experts will know, he published the first serious piece of scholarship, 'Studies in the Literature of Sherlock Holmes', in 1911. He even gained the attention of Arthur Conan Doyle.

I did not move in the same fashionable circles as Monsignor Knox. I had more or less concluded my period at Oxford when his paper was delivered as an address to the Gryphon Club. And as I had when I saw the Gillette play six years earlier, I was somewhat chagrined to find my own interest given over to public posterity. Personally I was somewhat aggrieved to read of his idea that Watson fabricated the post-Reichenbach Falls Holmes cases to supplement his spendthrift income, but obviously Knox was writing with tongue-in-cheek wit. Sadly, many of his later adherents took the rule of this game all too literally, and treated it with a pompous seriousness akin to Holy Writ.

I passed some clear Gryphon Club acolytes one day, pontificating at length in the quadrangle. It was a fine summer's day and they were poring over that familiar-looking Newnes paperback of *The Return of Sherlock Holmes*. "Quite clear that Watson had to fake the later ones. Or worse, that bungler Conan Doyle."

"Well, you know Doyle couldn't get a detective story right. After all, where was that Jezail bullet again, Arthur? Was it in Watson's shoulder or his leg?"

The others laughed at this badinage, but I could take no more of it. I stepped forward to confront them.

"You silly people!" I declared. "To take such sport with something that was meant for nothing but enjoyment—it is so heartless! And rather witless as well, I should add!"

As one might expect, these men were quite withering to me. Their sneers were expressed in the usual Oxford way—a disdainful and dry dismissal.

"This is exactly why women scholars will never amount to anything in Oxford," one of them said. "A classic example, one might say."

"Quite," the other, even more chinless fellow, asserted. "Here we are having a cogent and empirical scholarly debate, and she comes charging in, all full of sentiment and tears."

I had taken the time in this immature discourse to collect myself. My reply was thus a cooler and more considered one than my introduction. "What a shame you are as short-sighted about progress as you are about your Holmes facts. I know for a fact that Watson did not fabricate the post-Reichenbach Holmes stories."

As the words tumbled from my mouth, I regretted them. For I was now stuck between either having to explain my real identity—something that, for this exact kind of exchange, I had not wanted to get around the university—or shuffle off and seem as silly as these nitwits wanted me to be.

As it was, an irate tutor of about ninety came outside and castigated the ringleader of the odious gang. "You were supposed to report to my digs twenty minutes ago!" he fumed. "No wonder your Greek is so appalling with that dozy attitude. Talking about your Holmes fairy stories again, I shouldn't wonder!"

The ringleader reverted still farther to his childhood, sulkily declaring, "They're not fairy stories. Haven't you heard Monsignor Knox—"

"I'm fed up to high heaven with Monsignor Knox," the tutor sighed. "We study serious subjects here at Oxford, not penny-dreadful modern drivel. Now come alone, you young oik!" He then seized the man—by the ear, for an added touch of deserved infantile humiliation—and dragged him through the quadrangle.

"Best of luck with your Classics!" I called to him as he receded into the distance.

For all the chauvinistic frustration I felt at the time, I came to regard that day as a nostalgic, glowing window into that time. For, I sometimes chill to think, many or all of those callow and feckless young boys—who had nothing more important than to argue over Holmes and play truant—would be charging through mud in France, plummeted from that gleaming and rarefied Edwardian utopia into the most sordid Hell the twentieth century could conceive for them.
**

By 1915, when I was twenty-and-six (the same age Mother had been when Father first came into her life), the fourth Sherlock Holmes novel, *The Valley of Fear*, was serialized in the *Strand Magazine*. Time had now made my constitution bitterer. The Great War was in its full and terrible throes, and I had taken some limited medical training, so as to lend assistance to the throngs of soldiers so massively and senselessly maimed and killed in that endless and fruitless conflict. It was touching to see Arthur Conan Doyle's vocal patriotism had not lessened over the years, although his words were hopelessly naïve and ill-informed in light of this barbarous mayhem. With that as a background, re-acquainting myself with the Victorian nostalgia of Holmes's world was at first, as I am sure it was to many millions of readers, a welcome and pleasantly nostalgic diversion. Its first chapter, certainly, struck me as noticeably better than the rather listless Holmes war story, 'His Last Bow' (even though I was amused to note that Holmes had adopted the same alias, Altamont, he took the last time I had seen him).

However, as the months passed and the chapters regularly appeared in the *Strand*, this initial enthusiasm sharply deteriorated. Especially in light of reading in Mother's diaries how it had become something of a fascination for her, I found *The Valley of Fear* all the more curiously stodgy and un-involving reading. Holmes and Watson barely put in an appearance, and the second part with its Irish secret society seemed somehow like an inferior version of Arthur Conan Doyle's *grand guignol*

218

Mormon prequel in the second part of *A Study in Scarlet*. And the story seemed to end just as it was getting going, with Professor Moriarty's part connecting the two sections of the story unresolved.

I wondered, too, how Holmes scholars would resolve the presence of the Professor with Father's claim not to know of him in 'The Final Problem'. It was a decision clearly made when he expected that earlier tale to be the last published Holmes adventure, but made the whole narrative seem tenuous and arbitrary. I had become a very demanding reader, I see now—but I believe these demands were the ones that Watson and Conan Doyle themselves created with their obsession over details, laying the gauntlet down for future readers to pick apart and draw their own conclusions. *The Valley of Fear*, by such a reading, was a decent enough thriller, I concluded, and it was only because of the (impossibly?) high standards to which I had elevated Father's work that I found it wanting.

My nursing experiences were not on the whole notable—I was only doing what I could, and I believed the bravery of the men who were admitted far outstripped my own part in their recovery. The most notable soldier whom I nursed to health came in nearly at the end of the war. He had sustained a quite awful shrapnel injury a few months earlier, and was admitted to us in a state of shell-shock from the recent battle. After a painful and lengthy operation, a piece of embedded shrapnel from his earlier wound was extracted. All through his treatment, he kept looking up at me, pressing his bloodied hand to my face and desperately declaring, "I know you! I remember you!"

Of course, similar professions—and even more delirious admissions—were common amid the horrible experiences the men faced in battle and in operations. I was accustomed to hearing them and nodding with sympathy, though obviously I took with a grain of salt their declarations that I was the kindest and most beautiful woman they had ever seen, that I had cured their wounds and made their pain go away with my warmth, and—the most embarrassing—the fellow who said he would leave his wife for me!

With this young, sandy-haired shrapnel victim, though, I found out he was actually correct. I only got a clear look at him with his face cleaned up, as he was discharged from the hospital. He was that drably-dressed man lingering around Baker Street when I had my unsatisfying interview with Martha! I had only caught his first name, though, and soon the infirmary was filled up with fresh victims of Lord Kitchener's savage idiocy. I thought of him often as the war went on.

At this same time, possibly inspired by the uncertainty of war that loomed so large over us all, Father's distant relations grew unexpectedly closer. Until that point, he had sent monthly stipends to Mrs. Forrester, and the occasional added gift around my birthday. He had also, as I mentioned, put forward on my behalf an application to study at Oxford. I was extremely grateful for this consideration, but I did hope that just once, he might have come into contact with me for more social purposes.

Anyway, when I turned twenty, the pattern of these welcome but somewhat cold obligations was surprisingly broken. I began to receive long and regular letters from him. In this correspondence, he expressed regret at his conduct with me, and quite how much time had elapsed. He had returned to practice to support his new young family, and I observed (deduced, as Holmes would say, even though 'induced' is probably the more correct term) that he was hoping to assume a more responsible patina as he approached his seventh decade.

I read these letters, I occasionally responded to them—but I was now much changed from the girl who had followed his writings with such youthful enthusiasm. Mrs. Forrester and I did not talk often about Father—as she grew older she preferred to tell me more of Mother and the friendship they had cultivated in those years before 1888. She particularly impressed on me that she admired Mother's independence.

"So many women of that time would do anything to take a husband. They'd marry some worthless sot just so they weren't 'left on the shelf'. None of that concerned Mary. She was always her own person, never needing or wanting anything but herself. Even though those pearls she was getting were her rightful part of an inheritance, she never felt she was owed anything by anyone. That's why I was so convinced that ... well, when she got married, she had made the right choice."

221

Through these observations, I began to take Mrs. Forrester's larger point, and became more and more convinced that I needed to carve out a life for myself, wholly independent of the past. In a way, Mother had inspired me—and though he was still alive, my father had no more closeness or bearing on my life than the absent, then dead, Captain Morstan.

We met again at Mrs. Forrester's funeral—which took place at St. Giles, the very cathedral where my parents married in that long-distant summer of 1888. It was by this point a few months after Armistice Day, in 1919. I was desperately bereft at the time. Her departure from my life was as soul-wrenching as Mother's, but I was now at an age for the full heart-ache to sink in. In a strange way, all the emotions I had not fully acknowledged at Mother's death came to the surface newly augmented by this fresh sadness. I now truly felt orphaned, and Father's presence was in this context, rather like greeting an impostor.

"You must have nearly finished your studies," he mentioned. "I know as a woman you won't be able to take your degree, but the study is the important thing."

I explained that, thanks to Trinity's *ad eundem* degree, I had joined the ranks of the 'Steamboat Women'. He was very pleased to hear of my accomplishment.

"I am grateful indeed to have the opportunity to thank you in person, Father."

Though I made some excuse, he insisted on making an arrangement to take me to dinner on an evening later in the week. "I cannot make my proper amends at a funeral."

"Amends, Father? You should not feel—"

"Oh, yes, I should feel that I must make amends. And I ask you most humbly that you at least give me the opportunity to try."

Therefore, we met again later that week in the Strand. I told him a little about my medical experience in the war. I tried to leave my feelings and anxieties out of the conversation.

"What are your plans for the future?"

"I had hoped Mr. Holmes might endorse my wish to become … to become a detective." Strange as it may seem, Father was the first person to whom I had admitted this ambition aloud. I had become yet more solitary in my maturity, and save for Constance, kept no particular friends from school or Oxford.

I was very heartened when he did not mock this dream, which in the cold and dreary days that followed that awful occasion, seemed so very childish and impractical. "I think you would make a fine detective. Holmes always thought your mother would have, and now the tide is turning. I do believe one day women will be able to do anything and everything men can. And not before time."

"I have also begun to consider … travelling abroad. Perhaps to Canada or America."

"Again, a wise choice. Those more modern countries have more opportunities for young ladies than are available in England. Although … no, I wish you the best."

"What is it Father?"

223

"Well … I do so deeply regret my actions, regarding you. I've come to feel that I abandoned you rather. Almost as bad, and despite my wishes and efforts, I ultimately abandoned Holmes as well. The agenda of a younger woman can be hard to refuse—harder even than Holmes leading me to an opium den."

I laughed. Somehow he had managed to relax my guard. "If you would rather I stayed—"

"Not at all. It was merely a foolish hope of mine that it could be belatedly corrected, but … I should under no circumstances stand in the way of your future now. I wish you every success."

Mrs. Forrester had also left me Mother's diary. For some reason this had mistakenly been sent to her nephew, who had only realized the error and sent it to me some ten years later. I somewhat resented her concealing the document from me for so many years, especially given the closeness to her I came to crave so dearly. It was only as I read it that I understood her perspective on it. I know from the lady that she would have left Mother's confidences to her daughter and never read the diary—but she must also have been somewhat conflicted about the potential emotions Mother might have expressed in her writings that were not intended for anyone else to know.

After Mrs. Forrester's death, I departed for Canada, and it was travelling through the New World that I began to work in the theatre. This was partly aided by the charming gentleman that I met on my passage across the Atlantic—

Roger Longacre. His entrance into my life has a somewhat miraculous feeling about it. For, in the most remarkable coincidence in my life, and the kind of happenstance that Sherlock Holmes always gained such gratification from— he was that drab-suited 'fan' who was standing outside Baker Street when I called on Martha for Holmes's endorsement, and whom I treated in the hospital during the War. The injury had not gone away, and he now walked with a limp and a cane.

"I was then a young and penniless writer," he told me, "and I was hoping that I could get Holmes or Watson to allow me to write a new play or a film script of their stories. But of course, I was too late. Seeing and overhearing your visit that day, I thought my luck might change if I introduced myself to you."

"And yet you did not until now?"

"Well …" he blushed. "I must admit I was utterly speechless at your beauty, and I could not bring myself to make the introduction."

I laughed at his self-effacement.

"As you can imagine, I kicked myself repeatedly for my reticence as the years passed. And then, when fate brought us together again, I was wracked with pain and hallucinating madly, with a shell sticking out of my leg! I'm sure you must have thought me a complete madman. I had only regained my senses after my discharge, and hadn't the wit to ask your name."

"I think, given the shell in your leg, I can understand."

"But to get to meet you a third time … it is more good fortune than I deserve."

I indicated the cane. "I'm not sure you did have such good fortune. You should understand though, that despite the training, being a nurse was not my real occupation. I really wanted to be a detective."

Meeting Roger, for the first time I saw my Holmesian resolve to remain unmarried could not be sustained. I do not consider it a weakness on my part, for I have been a stronger and more self-possessed person in Roger's company.

We married in New York, and spent many happy years in the theatre there. It was only the opportunity to follow a touring company back to England that made me feel, now that I was happily married, and indeed we were preparing to start a family, that I should lay to rest once and for all the ghosts of the past. We toured the regions of England for a year, which gave me more than enough time to prepare for my return to London, to see my father and properly discuss with him the emotions that had run so deep.

1926

At this period in my life the good Watson had passed almost beyond my ken. An occasional week-end visit was the most I ever saw of him ... My house is lonely. I, my old housekeeper, and my bees have the estate all to ourselves.

—'The Lion's Mane' (1926)

Watson closed the book slowly, and took a deep breath. A single tear rolled down his cheek, and he sniffed in self-conscious embarrassment. Several hours had passed in his reading, and not once had either of them spoken. However, both knew that they needed to stay there until this was finished.

Mary's visit to Queen Anne Street was her first encounter with him since she had left for Canada, and she filled him in on the intervening years. He did his best to conceal the hurt at not being present for Mary's wedding—that Watson stoicism was as present as ever.

"The theatre, eh? And that's how you met this, er, Roger?"

"Right."

"Well, I can observe from that fact, that you haven't quite given up on your dream of being a detective. I never quite got him to admit it, but I always thought from his love of disguise and frequent Shakespearean quotations that

Holmes had toured as an actor. Hm." He smiled without mirth. "So many years later … and still so much I don't know about him. So much I may never know."

"I may as well be candid with you, Father."

"Please, Mary—"

"No, it is very important. I suspect I have thought of you for far more of my life than you have thought of me. Whether that thought was the early love, the hero worship of yourself and Holmes, or the gradual disappointment I came to have in you before I left for Canada. When I began that new life, I was so very happy with Roger that I truthfully thought very little about my life here, and about my past. I had finally carved out a life for myself—Roger was obviously part of that, but the greater part was, through my career, finding my own voice as a person."

Dr. Watson cleared his throat, with just enough precision to show Mary he was holding back some emotion. "I tried to make amends, as you know."

"I do know, and I appreciated it, although it was too late by that point. Mrs. Forrester was wrong about you, I can see that from reading Mother's words."

"Mrs. Forrester never liked me, from the minute I barged into their Camberwell house covered in oil, having nearly been murdered with a poison dart."

Mary chuckled. Her father had not lost his off-hand descriptions of the most perilous occasions.

"Exactly. And Mother did love you so much. Sometimes, you must admit, you took advantage of that love. You made her feel forgotten. Her life was not as happy as it could have been."

Dr. Watson's fist slammed down on the desk. "Do you think I don't know that?" he roared. Mary was used to such outbursts, working in theatrical circles, and did not react. He took a long and deep breath, and regained his composure. "When I married—er, when I married for the second time, I felt a weight lift from my heart. In some ways those eight years after Mary ... after I was widowed, had seen me erase and deny the emotions that had run so deep. And so far, I have been married for twenty-four years, to a woman whom I love dearly. It felt like Fate had given me a second chance, a chance to take the responsibilities seriously. I grasped that chance wholeheartedly."

"People's lives don't merely stop and start again. You can't count happiness with one person as atoning for giving others grief."

"I know that, but truthfully ... there is no one I could love in quite the same way as Mary, as your dear mother. In part, I kept away from you because you reminded me so strongly of her. The emotions that brought up in me ... they were hard to deal with, so I withdrew from them, first by returning to the world of crime with Holmes, and secondly in the years of my marriage. And what I was going to say was that never for one second did I forget Mary, nor feel that anything that happened to her was anything other than my fault. That conversation I had with her—about what her life might have been like had she married Thaddeus Sholto. That concept still haunts me. If Mary were alive and with another person, no matter how wretched that would have made me in my loneliness, I would consider the happier than her being dead now. And the only way I can express these deep sorrows is through words that sound like false pieties spoken out loud. But please believe me that I so fervently wish it were so!"

He finally broke into tears. Had he written of such a thing happening in a Sherlock Holmes story, Mary would scarcely believe it was happening. Now that it took place in front of her, she crossed to the other side of the desk and took him in her arms.

"You are so … so very like her," he declared through his choking tears. "She would have been proud of the decision you have made, and more importantly, the person you have become."

"And as you know, I was always proud of the person you were. Even when it came to my own detriment." She kissed Watson's lined forehead, and he capitulated to the intimacy that initially surprised him. "And now that opportunity has brought us together again, and I can approach it on equal terms with you, I would like to seize it with all my heart."

"I hope then, that my few remaining years can in some small way set right what I had foolishly allowed to go wrong then."

It was some time later when Watson's telephone rang. "Hello? Yes, it's Ja—I mean, John. Yes of course, my dear. I shall be home directly. I just received a visit from Mary."

It was now very late, and Mary was expected by Roger. She talked airily of her plans, and she knew that Roger would be thrilled to meet her father. Perhaps something would come of their efforts, perhaps nothing would. Perhaps they would become closer and perhaps they would become more distant. At that moment though, with the spirit of potential and optimism in the air, Mary felt satisfied, and she suspected her father did too.

As she left the office, there was only one last thing Mary had to mention to Dr. Watson.

"You know, I went up to Sussex to see Sherlock Holmes."

"Why?" Watson did not know whether he was prying by asking this question. "I mean … when?" he added lamely.

"Last year some time, during the tour. Roger and I had gone through a bad patch. It was right before our wedding and everything just seemed to be … wrong between us all of a sudden. There was a little while last year when I didn't think I could trust him."

"Oh, I see. I am sorry to hear that." Watson cast his eyes guiltily away.

"Anyway, I didn't know who I could talk to about it. It was a time that made me really wished Mother had been around." After a pause of some length, she added, "I did think of talking to you about it too Father. But … I knew it wouldn't be the right circumstance."

Though she could see Watson didn't believe her, this was the truth. At that time, it would have felt to her like the gravest intrusion, bursting in on him and his new family—again, she felt like a relic. At that particular moment she did not want to feel that way.

"Anyway," she continued, "not knowing where to turn, I suddenly remembered the vague talk of Holmes having retired to Sussex. So I went down there, went to that little village he lives in, Fulworth I believe it's called. It was only when I arrived that I realized I hadn't the first idea about where he might live. I didn't think it would be too much of a problem though.

"I didn't count on the locals being as ... loyal as they were. I suppose they do it for their own protection as much as for his. Remembering Baker Street that day in 1905, I can't imagine how many tourists they get from all over, looking for Sherlock Holmes.

"Everyone I talked to said, 'No, Sherlock Holmes doesn't live here.' I then got a little more specific, saying that I was your daughter and I had known him when I was a child. Still they said they didn't know where he was. I suppose quite a few fans have tried that tack as well. I can't imagine how many supposedly long-lost relatives pop out of the woodwork every week."

Watson leaned forward through this, fascinated. Though he never said anything, Mary could tell from his attitude that he had never visited Holmes in his retirement. She could also tell that he dearly wished he could, but that the familiar distance of time had let that wish lapse and wither.

"Ultimately," Mary continued, "I decided to cut my losses and try the pub. It was a short walk away from the Seven Sisters, I can't remember the name. Rather shabby place, with a conspicuously surly landlord. I drank a pint and asked him a little about the area. I tried to ask with as little interest in my voice as possible. 'Any famous people live around here?'

" 'Not really,' he said tersely, then carried on washing a glass that looked as though it hadn't seen soap for many years. 'Some detective, they say. I never heard of him.'

" 'Oh really?' I said, affecting my greatest disinterest, but probably coming off worse than even some of my least trained actors. 'What's his name? I may have heard of him.'

" 'Barker,' he replied, looking up to see if that would get any reaction. I shrugged and shook my head. Someone, though, must have told him I was in town, and he had clearly delighted in toying with me. I moved away from the stool and over to the window.

"I sat facing the window, and I drank in silence for what seemed like quite a long time. I didn't want to leave straight away, as I'd had a long journey that was now for naught. I was still feeling quite emotional, and had only had gruff villagers to talk to all day. Still, there didn't seem much point in staying.

"Just as I was about to leave, I saw a familiar outline walking along the chalk cliffs. He walked speedily and with an intensity of purpose; this man was no everyday rambler. Even had I not seen the pipe and the outline of a pork-pie hat, I would have known who it was from that nervous, energetic gait.

"I ran outside, but the man was too far away from me. I saw him retreat towards a villa far away, which I could see no path toward. I wondered what had brought him down near the pub. Had he heard I was there? Was he curious who was asking after him this time? Had his brain further advanced over the years to having psychic powers?! If only he had come a little closer, seen it was someone who was actually known to him, I thought! I became quite mad with him for his carelessness."

Watson leaned further forward at her pause, and now that she had stopped talking scrambled for the most important question. "What was he—how did he—what did you see of him?"

"Nothing," Mary sighed. "Just that distant figure in the distance. The outline could have been a dozen men, and as I lost sight of him I thought I had let my imagination carry me away. Then, for a second, I thought I saw a second person—I couldn't tell whether it was a man or a woman—beckoning to him from a villa. But when I looked again, there was just him. He turned and looked down at the Sussex Downs. I waved like an idiot, struggling to get his attention. But it didn't matter. He just turned away and walked inside.

"But it wasn't the end of the world. Ten minutes later I was leaving Sussex, and by the end of the day I had managed to patch things up with Roger. We haven't had a serious argument since; it was quite miraculous.

"A few weeks later I received a letter, postmarked from Sussex, though there was no return address on it. It wasn't signed. The unnamed writer said that he had heard I visited Fulworth and was sorry for the rudeness of the locals. If I sent word to the pub that I was arriving, he would be there to meet me and would be happy to talk to me."

"Well?" Watson asked impatiently. "Did you?"

"No, I didn't go back. For some reason I decided I'd rather leave Sherlock Holmes as I had seen him that day. It didn't seem important to talk to him anymore, and even if I did, I'm not sure he'd have been any different than the person I saw off in the distance."

"How's that?" Dr. Watson asked.

Mary replied, simply: "Above us. And apart from us. And, ultimately, alone."

Bibliography

Adkins, Roy & Leslie. <u>Jane Austen's England.</u> London: Viking, 2013.

Barnes, Alan. <u>Sherlock Holmes On Screen: The Complete Film and TV History.</u> London: Titan Books, 2008.

Barzun, Jacques. "Introduction." In Doyle <u>Adventures</u>: vii-xix.

Campbell, Mark. <u>Sherlock Holmes.</u> Harpenden: Pocket Essentials, 2007.

Davies, David Stuart. <u>Holmes of the Movies: The Screen Career of Sherlock Holmes.</u> London: New English Library, 1976.

---. <u>Starring Sherlock Holmes.</u> London: Titan Books, 2007.

Doyle, Sir Arthur Conan. <u>The Complete Sherlock Holmes.</u> New York: Barnes & Noble Inc., 1992.

---. <u>The Adventures of Sherlock Holmes.</u> Toronto: Bantam Books, 1985.

Field, Amanda J. <u>England's Secret Weapon: The Wartime Films of Sherlock Holmes.</u> London: Middlesex University Press, 2009.

Flanders, Judith. <u>The Victorian House.</u> London: Harper Perennial, 2004.

Green, Jonathon. <u>Cassell's Dictionary of Slang.</u> London: Weldenfeld & Nicolson, 1998.

Haining, Peter (ed.). <u>A Sherlock Holmes Compendium.</u> London: Warner Books, 1994.

Herbert, Rosemary (ed.). <u>The Oxford Companion to Crime & Mystery Writing.</u> New
York/Oxford: Oxford University Press, 1999.
James, P.D. <u>Talking About Detective Fiction.</u> New York: Vintage Books, 2009.
Klinger, Leslie S. (ed.). <u>The New Annotated Sherlock Holmes.</u> New York: W.W. Norton
and Co., 2005-2006. 3 vols.
Knox, Ronald. "Studies in the Literature of Sherlock Holmes." In Haining 62-83.
Morley, Christopher. "In Memoriam Sherlock Holmes." In Doyle <u>Complete</u>: 5-8.

Also from MX Publishing

MX Publishing is the world's largest specialist Sherlock Holmes publisher, with over a hundred titles and fifty authors creating the latest in Sherlock Holmes fiction and non-fiction.

From traditional short stories and novels to travel guides and quiz books, MX Publishing cater for all Holmes fans.

The collection includes leading titles such as _Benedict Cumberbatch In Transition_ and _The Norwood Author_ which won the 2011 Howlett Award (Sherlock Holmes Book of the Year).

MX Publishing also has one of the largest communities of Holmes fans on Facebook with regular contributions from dozens of authors.

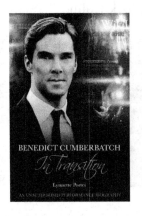

www.mxpublishing.com

Also from MX Publishing

 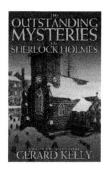 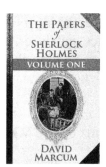

Our bestselling books are our short story collections;

'Lost Stories of Sherlock Holmes' , 'The Outstanding Mysteries of Sherlock Holmes', The Papers of Sherlock Holmes Volume 1 and 2, 'Untold Adventures of Sherlock Holmes' (and the sequel 'Studies in Legacy) and 'Sherlock Holmes in Pursuit', 'The Cotswold Werewolf and Other Stories of Sherlock Holmes' – and many more......

 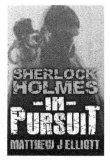 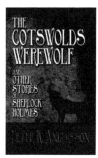

www.mxpublishing.com

Also from MX Publishing

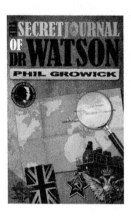

"Phil Growick's, 'The Secret Journal of Dr Watson', is an adventure which takes place in the latter part of Holmes and Watson's lives. They are entrusted by HM Government (although not officially) and the King no less to undertake a rescue mission to save the Romanovs, Russia's Royal family from a grisly end at the hand of the Bolsheviks. There is a wealth of detail in the story but not so much as would detract us from the enjoyment of the story. Espionage, counter-espionage, the ace of spies himself, double-agents, double-crossers...all these flit across the pages in a realistic and exciting way. All the characters are extremely well-drawn and Mr Growick, most importantly, does not falter with a very good ear for Holmesian dialogue indeed. Highly recommended. A five-star effort."
The Baker Street Society

MECHA- POTTER STRIKES!

CPSIA information can be obtained at www.ICGtesting.com
Printed in the USA
LVOW04s0502140215

426988LV00009BB/116/P